THE ROUGE OF THE NORTH

The ROUGE of the NORTH

by

Eileen Chang

University of California Press

Berkeley   Los Angeles   London

University of California Press
Berkeley and Los Angeles, California

University of California Press, Ltd.
London, England

First California Paperback Edition 1998

The University of California Press gratefully acknowledges the support of Cyril Birch, Hsin-cheng Chuang, C. T. Hsia, Karen Kings-
bury, Mrs. Stephen Soong, David Der-wei Wang, and P'ing Hsin-t'ao
of Crown Publishing Company, Ltd., Taipei, Taiwan.

Library of Congress Cataloging-in-Publication Data

Chang, Ai-ling.
    The rouge of the north / by Eileen Chang.
        p. cm.
    ISBN 0-520-21438-2 (hardcover : alk. paper)
    ISBN 0-520-21087-5 (pbk. : alk. paper)
        1. Married women–China–History–20th century–Fiction.
    I. Title.
    PS3553.H27187R68   1998
    813'.54–dc21   97-37526
                                                             CIP

1   2   3   4   5   6   7   8   9

The paper used in this publication meets the minimum
requirements of American National Standard for Information
Sciences–Permanence of Paper for Printed Library Materials,
ANSI Z39.48-1984. ∞

The face powder of southern dynasties,
The rouge of northern lands.

Chinese expression for the beauties of the country,
probably seventh century

FOREWORD

David Der-wei Wang

The Rouge of the North (1967) is the last of the three novels written in English by Eileen Chang (1920–95). Chang's two earlier English novels, *The Rice-Sprout Song* (1955) and *Naked Earth* (1957), were written during her sojourn in Hong Kong from 1952 to 1955, as part of an anti-Communist literary campaign sponsored by the United States Information Service. For all their compassionate inquiry into human frailty in an era of moral fanaticism, the two novels flaunt politics in ways Chang would not have chosen had she had any choice. Chang came to the United States in 1955, hoping to restart her career as a writer of English fiction, and *The Rouge of the North* came as the result of a long period of work towards that goal. Compared with the two earlier works, *The Rouge of the North* exhibits many more of the characteristics that made Chang the most popular writer in Shanghai during the 1940s. This is a novel not about national politics but about politics as a daily practice of life. It does not have the usual revolutionary "obsession with China," to use C. T. Hsia's term;[1] rather it probes the reactionary meaning of all such Chinese obsessiveness.

The story of *The Rouge of the North* revolves around the life of a woman named Yindi, from her coquettish youth to her shrewish and malevolent old age. Alongside Yindi's degeneration one sees the gradual breakdown of an old aristocratic family which Yindi marries into, against a backdrop of Chinese historical turmoil from the fall of the Qing dynasty to the last years of the Second Sino-Japanese War. Chang details the predicament of an old-fashioned household in a changing time, with moral and psychological consequences that amount to a macabre spectacle. Yindi's life is ruined by the stale environment which, ironically enough, she herself chooses. By agreeing to an arranged-marriage proposal from a richer family, she had intended to exchange her beauty and youth for a more affluent, respectable life, and when she finds out that her husband is a blind, puny invalid and his household a feudal dungeon, it is too late. After years of bitter experiences, Yindi is seen at the end of the novel as a rancorous widow, standing watch over her only son, whom she has totally depraved, in a tomblike house enshrouded with opium smoke.

If this plot sounds familiar to readers of Chang's earlier works, it is because except for minor changes in characterization and episodes, the novel derives from Chang's novella *Jinsuo ji* (*The Golden Cangue,* 1943). The novella was very well received, and Chang later translated it into English under the title *The Golden Cangue.* Similarly in the 1960s, when Chang was working on *The Rouge of the North,* she derived its Chinese counterpart, entitled *Yuan-nü* (Embittered woman). *Rouge* was published by the Cassell Company of London in 1967, when *Yuan-nü* had already been serialized for a year in literary media in Hong Kong and Taiwan.[2] A bilingual writer, Chang enjoyed a reputation of being able to rewrite or translate her Chinese works into English or vice versa,[3] but no other translingual practice engaged her so much as *The Rouge of the North* (or its ancestor, *The Golden Cangue*). Thus, over a span of twenty-four years, in two languages, Chang wrote this story four times.

The year 1967 was the turning point of the last part of Chang's life. In that fall, her second husband, Ferdinand Reyher (1897–1967), died after a long illness in Cambridge, Massachusetts, where she was writer-in-residence at Radcliffe College. Since their marriage in 1956, the couple had had a close but financially unstable relationship, and more often than not Chang became the major source of family income, taking on chores such as script writer for the Voice of America and for a Hong Kong movie studio. Chang never ceased creative activity, however. After the disappointing outcome of the first two attempts, her entry into the English and American literary market had become all the more urgent; publication of *The Rouge of the North* was therefore a crucial step in her career.

But the novel came out at an emotionally difficult time in her life, and worse, it was received coldly by both reviewers and general readers. Ironically, the Chinese version of the novel was warmly welcomed in Hong Kong and Taiwan, and in overseas Chinese communities, thereby rekindling "Eileen Chang fever" among Chinese readers for years to come. Chang subsequently gave up hope of becoming a professional writer of English and turned instead to work on several other Chinese projects. In 1969, through friends' arrangements, she left the East Coast for good, to become a researcher at the Center for Chinese Studies of the University of California at Berkeley. Two years later she had lost this position, and she moved to Los Angeles, where she began the final twenty-five years of an increasingly reclusive life.

⌗

From Chinese to English, from *The Golden Cangue* to *The Rouge of the North*, why did Eileen Chang keep writing the same story? Circumstantial factors may provide some explanations. After two disappointing efforts, Chang needed a novel to bring her the much-expected breakthrough. To that end a story such as *The Golden Cangue* seemed to contain the most promising ingredients: a woman protagonist, an orientalist allure, and a family-saga structure. More important, looking back at the success of *The Golden Cangue* among Chinese readers twenty years before, Chang must have concluded that a work of a similar nature should also appeal to her prospective Western audience. I even suspect that C. T. Hsia's critical appraisal may have confirmed Chang's decision. In his *History of Modern Chinese Fiction* (1961), Hsia took a then most unorthodox stance by celebrating Chang as a major writer of modern Chinese fiction up to 1949. His chapter on her centers upon a favorable analysis of *The Golden Cangue*.[4]

Beyond these contextual surmises, nevertheless, there must be something else that drove Chang to repeat herself, something more keenly felt that made the rewrite an artistic necessity. One can guess that years after leaving Shanghai, the ultimate source of her inspiration, Chang might have wanted to rescue her dimming memories of the beloved city by continually *naming* it. Thus Shanghai's meandering alleys, crowded, dilapidated bungalows, hybrid fashions, night cries of snack vendors, mixed smells of sesame oil, medicinal herbs, and opium, its festivities and rituals, courtesan culture . . . are fondly called up as the subtext of *The Rouge of the North*. Above all, Yindi's is a Shanghai woman's adventure; to write about her ups and downs is to recapitulate the changed morals and manners of the city during the first half of the twentieth century.

Or at a deeper, psychological level, one can draw on the Freudian model and view Chang's rewriting as a compulsive act that would overcome her own trauma by explaining it away. The four versions of *The Rouge of the North* (or *The Golden Cangue*) can be read as various accounts of her family romance, each revealing bits and pieces of a past from which Chang tried in vain to escape. The Yao family in *The Rouge of the North*, for example, easily reminds one of Chang's own, which enjoyed wealth and prestige in the late Qing days but underwent rapid decline after the founding of the Republic. Chang's father was a profligate consumed by opium, women, and memories of bygone family splendor. He led a life estranged from Chang's mother, a free-spirited woman who found solace by traveling overseas. When the couple finally broke up, Chang and her brother were left in the custody of their father and new mother, an old-fashioned, peevish woman and opium addict. At the age of sixteen, after a quarrel with her stepmother, followed by her month-long imprisonment in her own room and a devastating attack of malaria, she ran away from home for good. For Chang, images such as the moribund household, dissipated male family members, absent mother, evil stepmother, and decayed aristocracy that fill *The Golden Cangue* and *The Rouge of the North* are not merely literary motifs; rather they are figures symptomatic of the uncanny "return of the repressed," continued linguistic approximations of an unspeakable trauma.

What concerns me here, however, is not the extent to which Chang has retrieved or revised her repressed memories through storytelling. Literature need not serve merely as reference to authorial turmoil. Instead of tracing out the apparent similarities between *The Golden Cangue* and *The Rouge of the North* and identifying in them the imprints of Chang's lived experience, I argue that the differences underlying the seemingly repetitive writings provide more clues to Chang's desire to retell her story. In other words, in her effort to reconstruct the master plot through various forms, Chang may also engage in a more subversive activity by proliferating and therefore undermining that master plot. The rewriting project becomes all the more intriguing when one considers the issue of language and translation. As if she could no longer trust her mother tongue, Chang seeks a substitute voice—in this case, English—in which to communicate. A foreign language was no more alien a medium than Chinese to transmit, or translate, her already alienated

xi

existence in the Chinese environment. Insofar as mimetic realism was the most important format of modern Chinese fiction, Chang's repetitive and bilingual project has offered a special perspective from which to view such premises as thematic and linguistic authenticity. They point to her unique stance as a woman writer as well as her philosophy of writing.

When *The Golden Cangue* was published, Chang was a single woman writer of twenty-four. The novella brought her unexpected acclaim from critics such as Xunyu (pseudonym of Fu Lei) and Hu Lancheng (1905–81), the flamboyant literatus and collaborator during the Japanese occupation, and to a large extent it led to her romance and eventual marriage with Hu. A story about the transformation of a woman named Qiqiao from her frustrated youthful days to the moment when she has become a miserly widow and vampirish mother, the novella excels in its unsentimental exposé of women's fate in the traditional family system and in its intricate narrative skill, which superbly fulfills the standards of high realism. Next to Lu Xun's Madman in "The Diary of a Madman," Qiqiao must be the most memorable "madwoman" in modern Chinese fiction testifying to (what Lu Xun calls) the cannibalism of Chinese society. Suffice it for C. T. Hsia to say that "*The Golden Cangue* [is] the greatest novelette in the history of Chinese literature."[5]

While *The Rouge of the North* derives its story from *The Golden Cangue*, one finds interesting differences in the way Eileen Chang relates the plotline. Although she is a woman just as deeply disappointed by life as Qiqiao, Yindi appears a milder and therefore arguably more mediocre version of her counterpart. Where *The Golden Cangue* with its novella format highlights only the moments crucial to Qiqiao's life, *The Rouge of the North* traces every twist and turn of Yindi's moral and psychological degeneration. The result is a prolonged account filled with details, details which discharge the intensity of the original story and as such make the characters fuller and yet less compelling creatures. In *The Golden Cangue*, for example, Qiqiao's desire for her brother-in-law, Third Master, is only suggested in a scene of mutual flirtation. In *The Rouge of the North*, one learns how Yindi once sang a ballad to Third Master in the dark at night, had a frustrated rendezvous with him at a Buddhist temple, and tried to kill herself afterward out of shame and fear. Qiqiao later schemes to ruin her son's and daughter's marriages, and toward the end of the novella she is seen confined to her opium couch, all by herself, awakening only momentarily to the horror of her perverted existence. Yindi has only one son. Like Qiqiao, she manipulates her son's life and is responsible for his wife's death, which is followed by an irony: she ends up having to live with her son's vulgar concubine and a group of totally unlikable grandchildren.

C. T. Hsia's analysis of Qiqiao would sound equally persuasive if applied to Yindi, a woman embittered to the point of perversion by her surroundings. But critics have pointed out that Yindi is lacking in the kind of vengeful determination and manic energy that make Qiqiao the most villainous mother in modern Chinese literature.[6] For a story whose power depends on its protagonist's irreconcilable resentment of the world and people around her, Yindi may indeed appear to be a less successful creation. Eileen Chang, however, would have argued differently, and her reasoning might very well have been based on her polemical concept of realism. Take a look at her famous statement in "My Own Writing," written in the 1940s:[7]

There aren't many people around who are either enlightened or perverse to an extreme. This is a troubled era that does not allow for any easy enlightenment. In these years people have just gone on living and even though insanity is insanity, there are limits. So in my stories, with the exception of Cao Qiqiao in *The Golden Cangue*, none of the characters are extreme. . . . They have no tragedy, just desolation.

Chang wrote these remarks in response to charges that her works were not realistic enough to reflect the ethos of the time. As the mainstream discourse of the post-May Fourth movement, realism by the 1940s had become a codified dogma informed by various ideological and emotive imperatives. As Chang intimates in the above quotation, this realist discourse disguises both a high-strung sentimentality and a radically heroic call to arms. For Chang, realism lies instead in the territory where heroism is susceptible to compromise and revolutionary postures are struck for private, often trivial motives. Quite contrary to the common wisdom, she contends that realism can best exert its power by depicting not extremities but expediencies, not life as tragedy but life as desolation.

Qiqiao of *The Golden Cangue* harbors an extraordinary rage and delusion and shows no qualms inflicting these upon her closest family members; she induces our pity and fear, in the tragic vein, in that her fall shocks us to an understanding of her pain and vengefulness. A powerful figure she may be, nevertheless her portrait is one Chang's aesthetics of desolation would not endorse. It is Yindi, with her entanglement in the redundancy of life and her insufficient attempts in protest against that redundancy, who brings forward the vulnerability and mediocrity in us, flaws which are all too human. Such a view may raise some readers' eyebrows, and the debate over the *The Golden Cangue* versus *The Rouge of the North* will continue in the foreseeable future. My point is that between Qiqiao's malice and Yindi's bitterness there exists a whole range of emotional capacities, and that it took Chang more than two decades to transform her Qiqiao into Yindi, or to turn a tragic monster into a desolate woman.

At a time when most Chinese writers engaged in a resolute rendition of typical characters and epic subjects, Chang's preference for the desolate aspect of life already bespoke a personal agenda. Her realistic project did not stop here, however. Insofar as modern Chinese realism was based on a mandate to reflect—duplicate without altering—the real, Chang's effort to double, nay, to quadruple, the reflection came as an intriguing critique of the conventionally simplified view. In view of her vivid assemblage of detail drawn from all aspects of life, one might easily conclude that Chang's rewriting of the prototype of Qiqiao/Yindi amounted ultimately to more fully re-representing the same reality, or to reflections of one reality from different distances and angles. This view would tend to overlook the deliberately unrealistic aspect of her project. Consider Chang's own observation:[8]

> In this era old things break apart and new ones emerge. But until the era reaches its apex, earth-shattering events will be the exception. People only sense, to the point of terror, that things are not quite right in all aspects of their daily lives. . . . In order to prove their existence and grasp something real and quite elemental, they have no choice but to draw from their ancient memories for help, memories lived by all humanity in all eras.

In other words, when history has already crumbled and reality faltered, realism defined consensually has lost its legitimacy. In quest of alternatives, a conscientious writer can best express herself not by confronting or even prescribing actualities but by taking shelter in "ancient memories." Instead of proclaiming the irreversibility of time or the authenticity of action, as most of her peers did, Chang turned to involuntary memories, and willed repetitions prevail over reflections of empirical reality.

Gilles Deleuze once differentiated two levels of literary representation: "The first exactly defines the world of copies or of representations; it establishes the world as icon. The second, against the first, defines the world of simulacra. It presents the world as phantasm."[9] Most readers will have no difficulty appreciating Eileen Chang's realism at the first, mimetic level; all her works bear witness to her talent in recapitulating the world in its utmost intricacy. But I argue that Chang distinguishes herself more for her realism at the second level. She shows that the world we so confidently inhabit may already be a phantasmagoric existence, devoid of any solid meaning, and that any textual representation of it ends up becoming part of a chain of ghostly reflections. Her favorite subjects always involve ghostlike figures inhabiting a reality which no longer is, or never was, true. More important, her style betrays a futile inquisition of the immemorial and the unrepresentable, all the while impressing with its spectacular grappling with sensory, tangible data. Thus, in her own words, "a strange feeling toward surrounding reality emerges, a suspicion that this is an absurd, ancient world, dark and shadowy, and yet bright and clear. Between memory and reality an awkward disharmony frequently arises, and because of this a disruption—at once heavy and light—and a struggle—serious, yet still nameless—are produced."[10]

It is in this light that Chang's rewriting of *The Golden Cangue* and *The Rouge of the North* came as a truly fascinating project. The two works, together with their Chinese versions, beget each other's causes and effects, and as such they break open multiple entry points onto the real within the mimetic closure of representationism. In Walter Benjamin's words, "the important thing for the remembering author is not what he experienced, but the weaving of his memory."[11] While the majority of Chinese writers from the 1940s to the 1960s were eager to carve out the lucid image of their time and its single future, to have their say about what reality is and will be, Eileen Chang took a wholly different direction, by returning to her past and by letting it repeat itself, unwoven and rewoven in memory. Instead of the bright and clear worlds of May Fourth enlightenment and revolution, her works describe the dark realms of memory and desire, realms where ghostly interchangeability and duplicity prevail. Unsurprisingly, her philosophy of the real had to be acted out as a lifelong task. In the mid-1960s, when Chang tried again to tell the story of *The Golden Cangue* two decades after its first publication, she had aligned herself with such masters of recapitulation as Tanizaki Junichiro of *The Bridge of Dreams*, Marcel Proust of *Remembrance of Things Past* and, above all, Cao Xueqin of *The Dream of the Red Chamber*.

※

For all her concern about an age in transformation and a city—Shanghai—in decline, Eileen Chang makes *woman* and her status in the Chinese family system the central issue of *The Rouge of the North*. Yindi appears at the first as a saucy and resourceful girl, determined against all odds to seek her own marriage. Her parents already dead, she lives with her brother's family, which makes a living selling sesame oil. Yindi falls in love with Young Liu, an apprentice of the herbal medicine store next door, but she is wary of the predictable, poor life ahead of her were she to marry him.

Thus when approached by the go-between on behalf of the rich and powerful Yaos, she agrees to the marriage proposal as the result of pragmatic considerations. Little does she know that her future husband is a blind, puny invalid, one of the living dead, and that the Yaos' household is stifling and decadent. The rest of the story traces the consequences of Yindi's decision: her humiliating position among the in-laws, her sexual frustration with her husband, her increasingly haughty manner born of self-defense, her fruitless affair with her brother-in-law, Third Master, her widowhood, and her last metamorphosis as miserly tyrant.

For feminist readers, *The Rouge of the North* may appear to be a conservative novel, one which exposes the misery of Chinese women but fails to provide the necessary enlightening passages. Compared with contemporary women writers such as Ding Ling (1907–86) and Xiao Hong (1911–42), Chang shows little intent either to record or to imagine revolutionary alternatives for Chinese women. Under Chang's treatment, Yindi would at first glance hardly seem designed to win sympathy. Motivated by pragmatic considerations, Yindi *chooses* to bow to convention midway through her decision to fight for her right to choose. Worse, as if she had not suffered enough on her own, she later emerges as the most stubborn defender of the old customs and sees to their implementation in her son's and daughter-in-law's life. She subjects herself to a system which first victimizes her and then converts her to victimizer. (To borrow Lu Xun's popular metaphor, after being served up at the cannibalistic banquet of Chinese feudalism, Yindi develops her own taste for human flesh.)

As a character who fails to exit the vicious circle imposed on Chinese women, Yindi may seem best taken as a negative example, illustrating the triumph of a male-centered social machine. A closer reading, nevertheless, induces a very different interpretation. Chang may not be a feminist writer informed by "correct" consciousness, but throughout *The Rouge of the North* she never stops contemplating Chinese women's predicaments and the possible ways out. For Chang, Yindi's tragedy lies not in her acceptance of her destiny but rather in her wish to transgress its boundaries. Born with a shrewd, snobbish nature, she tries hard to transcend her milieu, and when she accepts the Yao family's proposal, she demonstrates the kind of self-expectation and unscrupulousness found in many a naturalist heroine. But as Chang would have it, Yindi calculates to no avail before spinning the treacherous Wheel of Fortune; her option of marrying either her beloved Young Liu or the invalid son of the Yaos proves to be a false one. Although in her old age she has every reason to regret the waste of her life, Yindi is aware nonetheless that the roads not taken led only to other forms of frustration and death.

Critics can call Yindi a coward, who quickly reconciles herself to society once she finds herself caught in its snares. Chang would not have thought so. While she might well salute those heroines who break the bondage of society and start a life anew—just as she did—Chang knew only too well that most Chinese women of her time had neither the skills nor the resources to change their own destinies. These women deserve a voice on their behalf. One can imagine that when Yindi joins cannibalistic male feudalist society, she is undergoing as painful a rite of passage as a woman who flagrantly exits from it in search of her modern selfhood; more so, if one recalls that she did not initially belong to a social stratum that could underwrite such a quest. Yindi's bitter success thus leads us to ponder the question: If it is not easy to become the New Woman in a traditional society, wouldn't it be at least equally trying to be a (self-imposed) traditional woman in a New Age? Yindi remains a last guardian of the Chinese family tradition when all her relatives have given up its already dated manners and rituals. Her eccentric conservatism partakes of a fanatic fervor which, with a deft reversal of the direction of history, would easily be recognized as radicalism. Not unlike certain female characters in late Ming storyteller tales, Yindi attains an unlikely existential prominence in a historically suffocating environment, not by defying its already obsolete values but by obeying them to the extreme.[12]

From Yindi's story one extracts an important feminist notion which we may attribute to Eileen Chang. Though less utopian than some of those recently in fashion, this notion can contribute to the debate on how to interpret the historical evidence of female victimization in view of modern women's desire for female agency. Chang of course means to make Yindi showcase Chinese women's degradation in a premodern world. But instead of promoting an across-the-board female victimology, she contends that such a subjugated position does not necessarily translate into virtue. Innocent suffering does not constitute grounds for sanctification. Yindi's story implies that whenever they are given a chance, women can prove to be just as cunning and conspiratorial as men. Women are as capable of oppression as men are, including the oppression of their own kind. There could be no feudal victimization without feudal women to prepare for, control, and administer most of it. In Chang's own words, from her essay "On Women," "thanks to the confined space allowed to their activities, perfect women can appear more perfect than perfect men, while villainous women can be more thoroughly villainous than villainous men."[13]

One could retort that a woman like Yindi after all is coopted by male power and that she pays a far greater price for what she becomes. Chang could not have agreed more, while perhaps adding that precisely because she understands women's disadvantageous situation so well, she has to pay due respect to the ways by which they survive male coercion, however infamously. The Yao family is headed by the dowager-empress-like Madame Yao. Witness the way she manipulates her sons in the name of the male-centered domestic ideology, and one realizes that Yindi is but a derivative version of the old matriarch. Through their collusion with men, women appropriate men's power and turn it against them. In other words, Yindi's story calls attention to the fact that unless women could be no less selfish, cruel, and energetic than men, there would not have been a chance for (some of) them to turn the tables and oppress their male oppressors, to say nothing of someday overturning all the institutions of male oppression. *Rouge* may appall us with Yindi's degradation, but the flip side of it indicates the fiendish persistence of women's power, which could be turned to other ends, in other societies, if not in Yindi's.

Chang's logic, to be sure, takes on a Machiavellian dimension and thus does not fit the consensual scenario ascribed to Chinese women of bygone days. For post–May Fourth humanists as for contemporary fundamentalist feminism, Chang's women characters are neither weak nor helpless enough to symbolize their abused status under traditional circumstances. But this is exactly the point Chang tries to make over and again in her fiction and essays: her women are earthy unscrupulous survivors, not honorable tokens.[14] In the battle between men and women, nobody leaves with clean hands. Alongside Yindi's dehumanization, all the male characters also undergo their own cycles of failure. Yindi's husband is a human skeleton and dies young; her brother-in-law, Third Master, ends up living off two prostitutes-turned-concubines; Yindi's sole son appears to be totally demoralized by the novel's close, thanks to his mother's fervent moral teaching. By portraying Yindi as both vulnerable and dangerous, both a victim and a victimizer, Eileen Chang has complicated the terms of gender politics and celebrated female power in her own cynically honest way.

⚬

Granting the contributions to the debate, one recognizes nonetheless that Yindi remains an unhappy woman and that this emotive state constitutes the most poignant aspect of Eileen Chang's inquiry into a psychology of women. The title of the Chinese version of *The Rouge of the North*, *Yuan-nü*, is in many ways more suggestive of Yindi's state. The Chinese character *yuan* denotes such meanings as "embittered," "sullen," and "rancorous;" when used to describe women, it refers to a major trope in classical Chinese poetic invocations of the feminine. Yindi's is thus not one woman's story; rather it reminds one of thousands of Chinese women who have been so deprived by their time and environment as to wither away in chronic distress. In contrast to masculine rage or wrath, Chang sees in women's simmering embitterment a menacing force, which often threatens their own well-being before it endangers society as a whole. Throughout her life Yindi tries to seek outlets for her deep-seated frustration or *yuan*—by marrying a rich husband, by her rendezvous with her brother-in-law, by fighting for family inheritance, by demoralizing her own son, even by trying to commit suicide. But to her chagrin (or *yuan*?) each of these attempts turns to have been another empty promise replacing the previous one, and her life amounts to nothing but a bitter spiral, closed in upon itself.

Critics in the vein of psychoanalysis cannot find a better case than Yindi's to address problems from depression to hysteria, from *ressentiment* to melancholy. Of all the syndromes readily to be identified, abjection is perhaps the one worthiest of consideration. Coined by Julia Kristeva, the term *abjection* refers to signs of repugnance as reactions to an inability to transcend the base associations of the corporeal such as food, waste, and gendered difference.[15] In contrast to the rational distinctions formed by (patriarchal) language and sign systems, the abject focuses attention on the "thresholds," which are manifested, among other ways, in those bodily orifices blurring the distinction between the inside and the outside, attraction and repulsion, Eros and Thanatos. While one could pursue Kristeva's theory further, my concern here is that abjection describes a feminine dialogue between desire and loss that resonates most intensely in "the ambiguous and the transgressive."[16] Yindi, I argue, occupies just such an ambiguous and transgressive position in coming to grips with her sexual and social identity. She wants to find her own man and yet is rewarded with a living dead man; she is torn by adulterous desire in her younger days, only to settle into her widowed life with formidable stoicism; she seeks to end her life in the middle of the novel, but outlives all the other major characters. Shuttling between the possibilities and impossibilities of her life, Yindi is never what she appears or wants to be; her transgressive desire continually throws her back into the closure of repetition.

But where Yindi eventually closes herself to the world in despair, Eileen Chang understands that something has happened. Where Yindi fails to articulate her pain, Chang is capable of naming at least the unspeakability of the pain. "Abjection appears," as one critic puts it, "where boundaries are traversed and unity punctured so that the resultant breach threatens to widen and overtake the whole."[17] This leads us to reexamine the scene which opens and closes the novel. In that scene, the teenage Yindi had been about to go to bed one night when she was disturbed by a repeated knocking at her door, with a man calling, "Miss! Miss!" Who was this man? What was happening outside the house in the darkness of night? Should she open the door? Almost unprepared, Yindi is pushed to the threshold of her life, so to speak, and she has to decide how to face up to the vehement pounding on her door. The door-pounding scene recurs at the end of the novel, in Yindi's remembrance of things past. The return, or repetition, of the youthful experience functions like a belated epiphany to Yindi, which sheds mysterious light on her life, though only in retrospect. Chang might have suggested that it bespeaks more emphatically the elusiveness of Meaning of any kind. Despite her eventful life, what happens to Yindi is really a repetition of her precursors' fate. The pounding at the beginning becomes an empty promise, with hollow echoes resounding throughout the narrative.

By repeatedly writing about a woman's abject experience in different forms and languages, Chang seems to have reenacted that door-pounding scene, trying to force open Yindi's world and to rethink the choices such women once had to make. And in view of Chang's own ambivalent response to Yindi's eventual fate, one wonders if she has projected her own drama of transgression and repetition. It is in this regard that Kristeva's interest in the linguistic underpinning of abjection theory lends special help. If language is that which is predetermined by the patriarchal symbolic order, the feminine presents itself as an amorphous semiotic force coming from outside the male order. This force continuously releases disruptive impulses into the symbolic while risking the fate of being expelled, which results in abjection. Women's writing in this interpretation is an unstable and provisional process, one that requires continued renegotiation, and reinscription, in its dialogue with the symbolic.

This tension is best dramatized in the climactic scene of *The Rouge of the North*, Yindi's liaison with Third Master. Yindi has followed the Yao family to a Buddhist temple in commemorative rites for the dead Master Yao. With her newborn baby she wanders into a courtyard where a huge iron urn stands:

> She wandered across the courtyard around the huge iron incense pot on its stone pedestal. Row upon row of names were engraved on it in small fine characters, donors who had this incense pot made, "Mrs Chan, née Wong; Mrs Wu, née Chow; Mrs Hsu, née Li; Mrs Wu, née He; Mrs Fung, née Chan ..." The purposely characterless names became a bit depressing seen *en masse*. These were the women who went in for good works pinning their hopes on the next incarnation. She had the feeling that if she looked more closely she would find her own name there, cast in iron. Maybe she had come across it without recognizing it.

This is a crucial scene because it is followed by the sudden appearance of Third Master. Should Yindi transgress the conventional boundary of feminine virtue by succumbing to the seduction of her brother-in-law? Or should she follow the model of those women who led a pious, decent life and let their names be molded *en masse* into the iron incense pot? Yindi chooses the first option. She follows Third Master to a side temple and is ready to give in, leaving her baby crying on a prayer mat. But Third Master stops right after he has aroused Yindi; the sexual encounter she has so dreamed of never comes true. Frustrated and shamed by the rendezvous, Yindi later tries to hang herself; her rescuer is the last person she wants to live for, her husband.

One can imagine that behind every small inscription of a

name on the iron incense pot, there is a story about a woman's embittered life; and for every woman whose name is being remembered there are hundreds of others who have been completely forgotten. Even the select few honored are known only by the names of their husbands. When she looks at the inscriptions and almost finds her own name among them, Yindi seems to have foreseen her own fate. But what follows this scene drastically undercuts the sullen implication of the inscriptions. I am referring not to Third Master's abortive seduction of Yindi, which is too obvious a contrast, but to the life Yindi leads long after the seduction. For all her youthful desire to break the law of virtuous womanhood, the aging Yindi becomes more and more pious and fanatical in her observance of established, patriarchal ideology. So it may not be surprising after all that she would yearn to be indirectly inscribed onto the monuments of patriarchal memory in return for obliterating herself on its behalf.

The way Eileen Chang describes Yindi's defiance of and spiteful conformity to conventional power thus may not be merely a deplorable case history. Rather it throws an ambiguous light, however unexpectedly, on the moral stature of those women who have had their names cast in iron. Insofar as their memories are all mere inscriptions, one wonders how many Yindis there must be among them, and, more poignant, how many others of them have carried on a complicitous relation with the male society that sanctioned them. The point is that these women may be *neither* naïve collaborators *nor* strong-willed martyrs living out male-centered fantasies. As Chang would have us surmise in the case of Yindi, perhaps their embittered life has trained them to *seem* and not to *be*: they may or may not have had a chaste and pious life, and yet they have managed to make men treat them as moral paragons.

By emphasizing the other side of Yindi's life, a life which once would have been cast in iron as a barely visible patronym inscribed upon a temple pot, Eileen Chang exhibits the most polemical part of her idea of feminine power. And to a great extent her strategy of writing, or rewriting, resonates with this message. Alongside her descriptions of Yindi's (or Qiqiao's) adventure, she sought within the May Fourth realist discourse a voice of her own, a voice that turned the programmatic enunciations about nation, humanity, and revolution into something else: she has blurred the nation, making it appear as alienation, making humanity show itself as femininity, making revolution devolve into involution. Above all, in contrast to the metallic, isolated inscriptions on the incense pot, Chang's narrative does not take congealed shape but lets its meaning float almost invisibly on its surface, like currents upon the water. Significantly, Chang entitled her famous collection of essays *Liuyan*: literally, *Floating Words*.

✁

We can now return to our starting point and rethink the significance of remembrance and repetition, transgression and translation, in the cycle of Chang's *The Golden Cangue* and *The Rouge of the North*. Through retelling the story of Yindi and her previous incarnation, Qiqiao, Chang rearticulates her own scattered memories and those of other women. And through reproducing the ghostlike images of Chinese women in abjection, she undoes the singular, essential discourse of realism as a *man*made myth. But more fascinating is the role translation plays in the cycle. Translation is a reiteration of the target language in a different medium, but it is at the same time a transgression, a violation as well as crossing of the linguistic boundary between what is decipherable and what is not.

Given Chang's background as a woman author with an

old-fashioned father and a Westernized mother, a bilingual and cross-cultural education, and noncommittal political grounding, translation becomes as much a syndrome as a strategy in her coping with life—inevitably, a way of making a living. To translate means not so much to bring to light the hidden meaning of the original, or father, nation, and reality, as to acknowledge its obscure status, which is "dark and shadowy, and yet bright and clear." Shifting back and forth on linguistic, cultural, gender, and temporal territories, Chang is able to find that "between memory and reality an awkward disharmony frequently arises, and because of this a disruption—at once heavy and light—and a struggle—serious, yet still nameless—are produced." This is a realm where the four versions of *The Golden Cangue* and *The Rouge of the North* are put forward in contestation and thereby the fates of Chinese women are renegotiated.

In the 1960s, when a feminist from the vanguard like Ding Ling had been completely silenced and exiled to the far north, Eileen Chang, self-exiled thousands of miles away from China, still carried on. As Chinese Communist politics precipitated the Cultural Revolution (1966), with an ever louder call for the coming of the new China, Chang withdrew further back into the dark territory of old China. Through rewriting *The Golden Cangue*, she indulges in "ancient memories," "memories lived by all humanity in all eras." A novel like *The Rouge of the North* became for Chang a last imaginary refuge after she had already taken political asylum in the United States. And in a circuitous way the novel provides a critique of the dominant literary discourse in her own country. It is a repetition in subject, but it has more to say about the old roots of the new era; it is a work in her second language, but it more emphatically transmits, or translates, her ideas about femininity and creative writing, which remain unintelligible to ideologues and party-liners. Chang has always occupied a marginal position in literature, as in (gender) politics, and enjoyed that position with an ironic sense; but there must have been moments when she had to come to terms with her own state of abjection. The 1960s were years when Chang drifted with her bedridden husband from one place to another, dreaming her last dreams of becoming a professional writer of English fiction, while her hope of homecoming appeared ever dimmer. One wonders, as she later reread *The Rouge of the North*, how often she must have been bemused, or amused, by an uncanny thought—that fictional experience had infiltrated lived experience, and that she herself might finally have become the embittered woman.

NOTES

1. C. T. Hsia, "Obsession with China: The Moral Burden of Modern Chinese Fiction," in *A History of Modern Chinese Fiction* (New Haven: Yale University Press, 1961), pp. 533–54.

2. Originally titled *Pink Tears*, the draft of *The Rouge of the North* was finished perhaps as early as 1958, as the result of Chang's project at the MacDowell Colony in 1956. See Sima Xin (Stephen Cheng), *Zhang Ailing yu Laiya* (Eileen Chang and Reyher) (Taipei: Dadi chubanshe, 1996), pp. 81, 98, 126, 138.

3. The other two English novels by Chang, *The Rice-Sprout Song* and *Naked Earth*, also have Chinese versions, respectively titled *Yangge* and *Chidi zhilian*. After the publication of the Chinese edition of *The Rouge of the North*, Chang went ahead to rewrite her two novels published after the Chinese Communist takeover of mainland China, *Shiba chun* (Eighteen springs, 1949) and *Xiao Ai* (Little Ai, 1951). The reason for these rewritings lies in her displeasure with the pro-communist messages she was forced to insert in the originals.

4. Ibid., pp. 398–407.

5. Ibid., 398.
6. See, for example, Hu Xin, *Zuihou de guizu* (The last aristocrat) (Taipei: Guoji cun wenku, 1995), pp. 442–49.
7. Eileen Chang, "My Writing," trans. Wendy Larson, in *Modern Chinese Literary Thought: Writings on Literature, 1893–1945*, ed. Kirk Denton (Stanford: Stanford University Press, 1996), p. 438.
8. Ibid.
9. Gilles Deleuze, *Logique du sens*, quoted from J. Hillis Miller, *Fiction and Repetition* (Cambridge, Mass.: Harvard University Press, 1982), p. 4.
10. Chang, "My Writing," p. 438.
11. Walter Benjamin, *Illuminations*, trans. Harry Zohn (New York: Schocken, 1969), p. 202.
12. For the conflict between individual commitment and social obligation in the Ming tales, see C. T. Hsia, "Society and Self in the Chinese Short Story," in *The Classic Chinese Novel* (New York: Columbia University Press, 1968), pp. 299–322.
13. Eileen Chang, "Tan nüren" (On women), in *Liuyan* (Floating words) (Taipei: Huangguan chubanshe, 1995), p. 88.
14. Ibid., pp. 86–91.
15. Julia Kristeva, *Powers of Horror: An Essay on Abjection*, trans. Leon S. Roudiez (New York: Columbia University Press, 1982), pp. 3–4.
16. Robert Newman, *Transgressions of Reading* (Durham: Duke University Press, 1993), p. 141.
17. Ibid.

1

Shanghai slept early in those days, already settling down at eight o'clock, the blue-green evening sky clearing as the sediments of darkness and hubbub slowly sank to the bottom. Electric lights were as yet uncommon in the Old City. The pebble-paved side street was almost pitch-dark with all the little shops boarded up for the night. The man had it entirely to himself. He weaved happily from one side of the street to the other, humming Peking opera with an occasional 'Ti guh lung di dung' to simulate the musical accompaniment. For coolness he had his pigtail piled on top of his head and his shirt open all the way down baring the chest. He fanned himself noisily in the back under the shirt with a palm-leaf fan.

He passed a shop where the large peep-hole was kept open to let in some air. There were voices inside but all one could see was a palm-leaf fan busily waving in the yellow lamp-lit square. It made him dizzy watching it. He walked on keeping close to the wall for support. There in the darkness he suddenly felt something cool and long slither down his back with a kind of swimming motion. He leaped high into the air and jumped again trying to shake it off. He turned around thinking that he would brush it off with his fan. It was only his pigtail that had come loose.

'Lay its mother!' he swore half laughing. To cover up his confusion in front of invisible spectators he flapped his fan loudly against his buttocks and swung into the slow measured 'square step', walking with feet wide apart, toes pointing outwards in the manner of mandarins in Peking opera, and sang,

'I, the king, drunk in the Peach Blossom Palace,
    With Han Su-ngo of beauty matchless.'

That reminded him. Turning around he looked about him and retraced his steps peering at all the familiar shopfronts until he came to the right one. He pounded loudly on the boards and shouted, 'Miss! Miss!'

'Who is it?' a man called out from upstairs. 'What for?'

'Miss! Miss I buy sesame oil,' he called out.

'We're closed, come tomorrow,' the girl snapped.

'Old customer, Miss!'

He kept pounding the boards. She finally came downstairs grumbling. Through the chinks between the boards he could see the light grow as she carried the lamp into the room. The wooden shutter over the peep-hole was pushed up with a clatter and he smelled a whiff of the pungent sticky juice of wood shavings that women put on their hair. Her face appeared and pulled back at once. The lamp shining up from under the chin had made the lips stand out bright pink and sculpted. It looked unreal at this close range looming out of a hole in the darkness and disappearing. But he knew it so well, the neat gold mask, a short face on top of the long neck and sloping shoulders. Bangs cut into a pointed arch swept down wing-like over wide cheeks, joined with the wisp in front of the ears that was plastered down to shape the face. A small purplish red mark stood like a spindle between the brows where she had pinched herself over and over again to pinch the heat sickness out of the system. She probably knew it was becoming as she was seldom without it all through summer.

'Hurry, pass me the bottle.' She stuck a hand out and he seized it.

2

'Let's hold hands,' he giggled. 'Let's hold hands, Miss.'

'Dead man,' she screamed, 'die from a thousand sword cuts!'

He giggled muttering to himself with quiet satisfaction, 'Sesame Oil Beauty'. They called her that in the neighbourhood.

She twisted her wrist about, knocking the silver-trimmed black rattan bangle on the edges of the peep-hole. He tried to pull out the trailing silk handkerchief tucked in the bracelet, which fitted so tightly he had trouble getting it out. She jerked back but his other hand held on.

'Take pity on me, Miss,' he whispered. 'I die from thinking of you, Miss.'

'Will you let go or not, dead man?' She stamped her feet and brought the flame of the lamp to his hand. The blackened dish of oil stood on a tall unpainted wooden stand. He almost upset it snatching his hand away.

'Ai-yo, ai-yo,' he cried. 'Miss, how can you be so cruel?'

'What's all this yelling?' her brother shouted from upstairs.

'The dead man grabbed my hand. Rotten corpse afloat! Corpse on the roadside. What do you take me for? Open your eyes and look, dead man.'

Her brother's wife poked her head out of the window. 'Gone. Who was it?'

'Who else but that dead carpenter? It would be my luck to run into a ghost today. Pig. Tramp, why don't you go and pass water and look into the puddle, see your ugly face.'

'All right now,' her brother called out, 'after all we're neighbours.'

'That's just it,' she shouted back, 'doesn't it embarrass him to come and make a row in the middle of the night

3

as if he doesn't know what sort of people we are? Next time he comes see if I don't hit him with the bolt. This time the tramp got off lightly. Born without eyes, dead man? May your mother be laid. Lay your ancestors eight generations back.'

She had got into the spirit of it. Her voice carried down the block. At last her brother spoke up again, 'All right, all right, don't yell, as if you're afraid people don't know. It's nothing that will give us face.'

'You want face?' she turned on him. 'You want face? You think people don't know what you do behind my back? Can you wonder people look down on me?'

'Still yelling. How is it a young girl has no shame?' Bingfa had already lowered his voice but Yindi raised hers another notch. The very mention of their quarrel had brought up all her anger.

'And you have shame? You've lost all of Father and Mother's face. So I'm shouting—if I didn't make enough of a row you'd have sold your own sister even. If I had known I'd never have shown myself. I felt so cheap and all your doing and you call me shameless?'

Bingfa leaned forward so suddenly his bare back sucked at the wicker chair with a light smack. But he was washing his feet, standing his long legs in a red-painted wooden basin with three feet.

'All right, all right,' his wife said, 'let her. After all a girl is a guest in the house. She'll soon be married and gone.' She dropped her voice. 'Marry her off quick. As the old saying goes, "A grown daughter is not worth keeping. Keep her, keep her and she turns into an enemy." And the way people talk, they'd say we want her to sit at the counter and draw crowds. A living signboard.'

He did not say anything as he wiped his feet with a shredded towel, grey with use.

4

'I tell you I'm really worried. There's bound to be trouble one of these days with all these men hanging around.'

He was alarmed. 'Why, have you noticed anything?'

'Well, like tonight. I have no time to keep an eye on her, so many children to take care of, otherwise I'd watch the shop myself, less worries all round.'

'Actually she would have done all right if she'd been given to the Wongs. They've just opened a branch at the Bridge of the Eight Immortals.' He jerked his head slightly in that direction.

'It's your fault really, it's for you to decide, how can you let her pick and choose? Without parents it's you the brother who gets the blame if she's not married. Next time you just have to be firm.'

He fell silent again. He would just as soon let it slide from year to year, there never was enough money for the trousseau, as if she didn't know. She looked at him. So did the red goose, all neck, which served as a handle to the basin. Carved in the flat on both sides, the profile reared up tall and straight in front of him fixing him with a concentric eye. He stepped into his cloth shoes, heels trodden down to make do as slippers. Feet planted far apart he turned away and spat. As if she had got her answer she picked up the basin by its neck and clumped downstairs on her bound feet to empty the water on the street outside.

She met Yindi coming up. Without a word Yindi backed down to let her pass on the narrow stairs. The little frame house was giving out all the heat absorbed during the day in fiery puffs. Yindi went back to her stifling room with a headache. She pushed back her wet bangs and opened her high collar, highest in front just under the cheekbones for a hollow-cheeked effect, with a

5

broad black trimming greasy and frayed around the edges. The side-fastened over-blouse came down to the knees, as tight as the trousers of the same blue glass cloth, all wrinkled. She felt under the pillow for a copper coin. Dipping it in a bowl of water she sat down in front of the mirror and scraped her neck with it, to scratch out the heat sickness. The square hole in the middle of the large coin gave her a nice grip. She scraped hard in long expert strokes, dipping it back in water from time to time. Three wide stripes of mottled purple and red appeared running alongside the throat. The bruised skin burned but she felt slightly eased around the heart. The nape of the neck should also be scraped but she could not do that herself and would not want to ask her sister-in-law.

The matchmaker was a friend of her sister-in-law's, an Aunt Wu. Bingfa's wife got to know her from clubbing together to raise funds once a month, each taking the pot in turn. Aunt Wu was good at getting people to join. She also sold lotteries, peddled enamelled trinkets and embroidered trimmings to rich families she knew, and made matches and delivered babies on the side. She had once worked as a maid. She got the Chais some business. A lady praying for a sick child had promised the god twenty catties of sesame oil a month for the eternal lamp. She had arranged for Bingfa to send the oil to the temple every month, as he still did in two jars slung from a shoulder pole.

This time she came to see Bingfa's wife one night and turned up again a couple of days later with two women in dark clothes with a northern accent. Yindi had thought it was strange the way they stared at her as they filed past the counter. Bingfa's wife gave them tea inside the shop but they did not stay long. When they were leaving she insisted on getting rickshas for them and called out to Yindi, 'Give me some change.' Yindi had no choice but to get money from the cash-box and come out from behind the counter. Everybody was standing in the street protesting. In the act of pushing back the money one of the women held her hands and looked at them, turning them over.

'Here, be careful, Miss, don't step into the puddle.' Aunt Wu bent down and lifted her trouser legs a little showing the feet.

She didn't like it. According to Bingfa's wife these were amahs of the lady who donated the oil to the temple. Aunt Wu had happened to bring them along. But Aunt Wu came again. Afterwards her brother's wife spoke to her for the first time about the blind son of a high mandarin's family. They were going to get him a concubine because of the difficulty of making a suitable match for him, so this one would be just like a wife. She realized that those two women must have been trusted amahs of the Yaos sent here to look her over, carefully inspecting her hands and feet as people did in shopping for concubines to see if there was skin disease and if the bound feet were small and well-shaped. She quarrelled with Bingfa and his wife for subjecting her to this. People were sure to think that she had been examined with her consent. When nothing came of it it would seem as if she did not pass the test.

It was true that her brother and sister-in-law had never thought of making money out of her before. She was the goods you lose money on, what they call daughters. At least concubines did not have to bring a trousseau. Even now it seemed to her that they did not think of her as a source of wealth but rather as an obstacle to their coming into a small fortune. Her position at home was getting to be impossible.

7

The men in the neighbourhood talked and joked about her behind her back but when they actually came face to face with her they seldom had anything to say. Sometimes they were bold like this carpenter who made trouble tonight. He would lean across the counter with a slight smile staring at her with eyes like two wet mouths. Filling his bottle she would set it down with a bang.

'Twenty coins.'

'Tch, tch! Why so fierce?'

Gazing into the air, her golden face impassive with the red mark between the brows, she suddenly spat out the words 'Dead man!' and turned her head aside giggling.

He went away vastly tickled.

This kind of thing would get her nothing but a bad name. She was already known as a flirt which was perhaps why matchmakers did not wear out her doorstep as one might expect, being called the Sesame Oil Beauty. Eighteen and not even engaged. With her own brother and sister-in-law plotting against her she felt like a fugitive carrying a jewel that endangered his life and was not marketable.

Tiny green insects flew around the lamp in droves, falling dead on the table with a dry rustle. Perhaps it would be cooler if she blew out the lamp. She sat in the dark fanning herself. Men are all alike. There was one who seemed a bit different though, Young Liu at the pharmacy across the street, tall, pale and as pretty as a girl in his long dark gown, not a speck of dust on his white cloth socks. It was a wonder how well-groomed he was, living in the shop with nobody to look after his things. She had often caught him looking across at her. Actually if he was not so timid he could have contrived to pay the Chais an occasional visit since he came from the same village as her mother on the outskirts of Shanghai.

8

Her maternal grandparents were still alive. When they came for visits they often dropped in at the pharmacy to bring him some message. He seldom had a chance to go home.

She went with her brother's family to see her grandparents during the New Year. They should have gone on the first of the first moon or the second or third at the latest, the days reserved for close relatives. But her grandparents were poor and partly dependent on Bingfa, so they did not have time for them until the fifth. They spent the afternoon at the village. Her grandmother mentioned that Young Liu was back for the New Year but had already returned to the shop. While she had not exactly expected to meet him there it disappointed her all the same. She felt bitter about her brother and his wife putting off the visit until the fifth. They are so snobbish, she said to herself. She made it out as if she was purely indignant on her grandparents' behalf. It would not be like this if Mother was alive, she thought and tears welled up in her eyes.

She had always liked the smell of a pharmacy, the acrid sweetness of preserved herbs chilled in the stone-paved large dark interiors. She went to buy medicine for her sister-in-law during her last confinement. Young Liu came forward with a smile and nod as if they had met and waited on her with lowered eyes, not saying much. She liked to watch him turn to the rows of little black drawers with set-in brass rings curled like a stylized cloud. He pulled them out one after the other, the householder in some fantastic home. The tiny scales stick and brass weights were like toys. When she got home she found wrapped with the other herbs a big package of dried white chrysanthemums that was not in the prescription. Several of these flowers soaked in a cup of hot water make a cooling summer drink. She was not too fond of the grassy

9

fragrance but she enjoyed making it every day watching the small white chrysanthemums plump out under water. She never had a chance to thank him. He would not want others to know that he had made free with the shop's goods.

That was all there was to it. She got up from her chair and stood at the window. A small illumined red square on the door differentiated the pharmacy from the other stores. They had kept their peep-hole open with a piece of red paper pasted over it and an oil lamp behind, illuminating the written words, *In emergency cases please enter by back door.* Somehow as she looked at the clear red square that would be kept aglow throughout the night, a vague sadness came over her that quieted the heart.

2

The boy selling oil puffs at a stall slept half-naked on the board where the dough was kneaded. The wire cage for holding the foot-long oil puffs stood empty near his head. The breakfast rush was over.

The street barber sat nodding on his stool. Aside from plaiting men's pigtails and shaving their front hair to get a domed forehead he also rented his towel and enamel basin to passers-by who wanted to wash their faces. With no business and with the afternoon heat upon him, he gradually sank forward in sleep, burying his face in the basin.

A hawker came with a flat pole on his shoulder loaded with bamboo chairs stacked mountain-high. He parked his wares on the shady side of the street, conveniently sat on one of those stumpy pale green chairs and went to sleep.

Yindi sat behind the counter under the vertical signboard that said in big gilt characters, *Children and old men not cheated*. Further out to her left stood another black-and-gold sign board, one of a pair that flanked the shopfront reaching down to the pavement, *Sesame oil from small grindstone, peanut oil and sesame butter*. She was edging a slipper with the kind of cross-stitch called 'mistaken to the end'. It had a nice tragic ring and the pattern of thin broken lines was more delicate than the usual dog-tooth. Her needle grew rusty from perspiration. Her eyes also felt gritty. The sun had got to the two big white enamel jars beside her with big yellow tongues of peanut butter hanging out. The buzz of the flies made her still drowsier.

She looked up and saw her grandparents coming,

holding palm-leaf fans overhead for shade. They must be in bad straits or they wouldn't choose such a scorching day to walk all the way here from the country. She was sorry to have to tell them that Bingfa and his wife were not at home, gone for the day with the children to the wife's family.

It always depressed her to see the red-cheeked timidly smiling old couple in their faded and patched blue garments. Without asking them whether they had had lunch she wiped the table, set out two pairs of chopsticks and went into the kitchen to warm the rice and the left-over dishes although it was already mid-afternoon. There was cabbage, melon and bean-curd. The tall wooden rice bucket was painted bright red with the ubiquitous goose handle rearing its flat head straight up, a round eye on each side. As she filled their rice bowls she patted down the rice so that it stood out of the bowl in a high mound round at the top. There were actually two bowls in one. Still her grandmother said, 'Press it, Miss, press harder.'

Husband and wife sat down facing each other and ate quietly. The blinding sunlight shone right into their faces but they seemed not to notice it in their heavy dream-like calm. Now and then their bowls and chopsticks tinkled faintly. Watching them she felt a little dazed and forlorn, like waking up dry-mouthed in the setting sun after a long nap.

They each finished three hard-packed bowls of rice. The old woman helped her to clear away the dishes while the old man napped in a chair, his fan over his face.

As they returned to the front of the shop after washing up they heard in the distance the thin flat twang of three-strings, the instrument played by blind fortune-tellers. The blind man was a long time in coming. The desultory music of the three-strings threaded in and out of the streets and alleys lined with black-roofed white houses, the little tune repeating itself winding in and out in a connected swastika design. For Yindi it called up a vision of her future set out like the plan of a town. Her hand went inside her blouse counting the copper coins in the pocket.

Her grandmother was also digging into her pocket. 'Let's call in the fortune-teller,' she said with a guilty little giggle.

'You want your fortunes told, Grandmother?' She decided that she would wait and see if the man got the facts right in her grandmother's past.

They waited at the door. The little street was mostly frame houses with open fronts, the worn brownish-red paint quite hidden by all the big lacquered signboards. The upper-storey windows seemed to bulge out with glass like dirty soap bubbles, yellow at the edges.

'Mr Fortune-teller!'

She hoped that their shouts would attract Young Liu's attention so he would know her grandmother was here. Maybe he could manage to slip over for a while and ask for news of home. But he seemed occupied at the pharmacy.

Ever since this talk of making her a blind man's concubine she had felt a kind of constraint, not unmixed with disgust, at the sight of the blind fortune-tellers in the street. She hung back a little as the man approached with his stick. The old woman took him by the elbow and helped him over the doorstep. He did not have a little boy to guide him around, probably because he was familiar with the neighbourhood. He was middle-aged, his sallow face was leonine with down-slanting ridges. Genteel and cautious, he looked like a tailor in his wrinkled long gown. And like tailors and all men whose profession subjected

13

them to women's whims, he wore the sour smile of patience taxed to the limit.

The old woman got him a chair. 'Sit down, Sir.'

'Ao, ao!' he answered, affecting the falsetto of the singing storytellers of Soochow. First placing a hand on the back of the chair, he lowered himself into the seat.

The old woman drew up a chair and sat opposite him, close enough to rub knees with him so she would not miss a word. After she had told him her date and hour of birth he mumbled to himself making some calculations. Then tuning up the three-strings he readily sang of her life, naming all the important events.

> ' . . . I figure in your fourteenth spring
> You lost your kind parent first thing.
> I figure in your fifteenth spring
> The red *luang* bird star was moving.'

Standing behind her grandmother's chair she tried to catch the lines rattling on with great rapidity. The kind parent means mother, the opposite of the severe parent, father. She understood that much and the star of the red *luang* bird is the marriage star. She did not know when her great grandmother died but she seemed to have heard that her grandmother had been engaged before birth, what was called 'pointing at the belly to make a marriage'. But she was not married early, so nothing could have happened at the age of fifteen. So this fortune-teller was no good. She was glad she did not waste her money on him. She thought it strange that the old woman did not seem aware of any mistakes. And she could not have missed anything; being an old hand at this she must be thoroughly familiar with the phraseology. She kept nodding her head encouragingly saying 'Um, um,' acknowledging the

14

various events with a smugly satisfied air as if everything had turned out just as she said.

Her two sons were both shiftless. He said she could lean on one of her sons and could look forward to ten years of 'old luck'.

'And then? What else?' she pressed, placidly insatiable. 'How am I going to end up?'

Yindi thought with some astonishment, at sixty-five she still thinks she will end up different from what she is now.

He sighed. 'It's a happy ending even if it's late in coming.' He sang another couple of lines repeating his promises.

'And what else? What else?'

Yindi felt ashamed for her when he said with an embarrassed little laugh, 'There isn't anything else though, Old Mistress.'

She paid him reluctantly and led him out of the shop. This time Yindi knew that Young Liu definitely saw them but he showed no sign of recognition. She was upset, wondering if he had heard anything about her, about those people looking her over as a prospective concubine. It couldn't be about the row with the carpenter that night?

'Your side gets all the sun,' said her grandmother. Was she comparing this side with the pharmacy across the street? Then she had also seen Young Liu. She did not greet him either.

'I wonder when your brother and sister-in-law are coming home,' she said. 'I want to speak to them about something,' she added importantly. She was so proud to have come to them on some business apart from borrowing money, she couldn't go away leaving it unsaid. There had been a struggle, she was not supposed to tell Yindi who was not to be told at all if the others were against it.

'Young Mr Liu's mother came to see us yesterday,' she finally said and Yindi understood at once. 'Young

15

Mr Liu is so nice, so quiet and good-natured,' she said half to herself. 'He's got a good job. Although they're not rich they'll always have rice to eat. They have very few people in the family, nice and quiet. His elder sister is married already and the younger one will be before long. The mother is easy to get along with.'

Yindi reached up to rub the needle on her hair and went on sewing.

'You are the only granddaughter we have, Miss. It would be nice to have you living near us. No use being shy. Poor child, you have no mother but you can tell Grandmother. It's all right to tell Grandmother.'

'Tell you what, Grandmother?'

'You don't have to be shy with Grandmother.'

'What's the matter with Grandmother today? I don't understand a word you say.'

The old woman cackled and was content to let the matter drop. She was clearly willing.

The fortune-teller was coming back after making his round. At the sound of the three-strings strumming far off she felt a strange sense of loss in the midst of her happiness. She need not wonder any more about the future. Her fate was sealed.

Somehow she had never thought of it from that angle, that she would be living with his mother in the country raising cabbages, in a yellow mud house surrounded by yellow mud smelling of night soil with here and there a tree misted by pink blossoms for a short while in spring. He would be home only for a few days out of the whole year. All year long she would be alone with the old woman and time, whose one idea was to make her an old woman.

Young Liu was not the pushing kind. He would probably remain a shop-assistant to the end of his days. They had clerks with whiskers in the same store, much respected. They wore long gowns while her brother with his messier job wore jacket and trousers like a labourer, but he owned his business. People would say it was a pity, she could have done better. Perhaps it was only natural qualms when it actually came to making an irrevocable decision, the more so because of the possibilities that all beautiful girls seemed to have, something incalculable about them. No matter how restricted, they may yet end up as empress or courtesan. She did not know exactly what it was that made her say, when her grandmother asked again what time Bingfa would be home, 'They won't be back for dinner.' The old couple could not wait that long. They decided to go home and come again the next day.

Bingfa and his wife returned with the children soon after they left and were none too pleased to hear that they had been here. Bingfa's wife remarked that they had come for money not so long ago. Throughout dinner she criticized the way they handled their money and let themselves be imposed upon by their no-good sons.

Yindi said nothing. She was heavy-hearted wondering how her brother and sister-in-law would take the Lius' proposal. What to do if they disapproved? It was one thing to put up a fight against a match and another thing to insist on marrying somebody. Of course there must be something between them. How far had it gone? Her sister-in-law was sure to make the most of it behind her back.

After dinner somebody banged on the door calling hoarsely for 'Sister-in-law Bingfa'. It sounded like that Wu woman. Coming just now it filled her with dread. How is it tonight of all nights? Whatever it is this time, it's going to make things that much more difficult.

Bingfa's wife hurried down to open the door. She sounded a little embarrassed and apologetic because of what had happened before but Aunt Wu was loud and hearty. As they came upstairs she even asked, 'Where's Miss? Gone to bed already? I'm getting to be famous as a matchmaker. All the girls run and hide wherever I go.'

She was dark and squat, freckled even on the arms, or were those 'longevity spots', the brown marks of age? Nobody knew how old she was. In her profession it was not so good to grow old. People began to wonder about your faculties and judgment. Her pop eyes stared seriously out of the round open face. The starch on her blue glass-cloth blouse smelled sour with sweat. When she came into the room where the light was brighter, Bingfa's wife saw she was wearing all her gold rings and ear-rings and at the back of her head a gold ear-spoon tucked into the little bun and a small red plush bat with a gold paper cut-out of the character *fu* stuck between its wings. *Bien-fu*, bat which puns with *fu*, blessings.

'You went to a wedding?'

'No, I've just been to the Yaos to wish their Old Mistress a happy birthday.'

'We've been out too, only just came back,' Bingfa's wife said.

'I came here straight after the birthday feast. Running around in this hot weather—I wouldn't do this for just anybody, to tell you the truth.'

'Yes, isn't it hot today?'

Aunt Wu demanded attention with a downward movement of her palm-leaf fan and raised her voice so that it could be heard in the next room; she did not trust them to repeat it correctly. 'It just happened when I was there today their young masters and mistresses came up to kotow to Old Mistress, and she saw that they all came in pairs. All except Second Master. So afterwards Old Mistress said, the second branch should have a wife too, otherwise it won't look right on such occasions. It doesn't

18

matter if the family is not well off as long as the girl is nice. So I said, in that case the Chai girl is just right.' She stuck her fan into the back of her collar and leaned forward to whisper, 'Old Mistress was not pleased. She said, Old Wu, you've been snubbed once already, do you want to be snubbed twice? After all there are plenty of girls in the world.'

The Chais could only smile.

She scratched the back of her neck with the fan handle. 'So I risked losing my old face; I said, Old Mistress, it just shows that the girl has character. She doesn't want to be a concubine no matter how rich and great the family is. As Confucius said, choose a wife for her virtues, choose a concubine for her looks. Not that this girl has no looks, I needn't boast, your own people have seen for themselves. And Old Mistress laughed saying, Confucius never said any such thing. But there is something in what you said.'

When she saw that the husband and wife still smiled saying nothing she leaned closer and dropped her voice, letting it rise again as she went on, 'Now I say a sentence only when there is such a sentence. This may offend you: Old Mistress said a shop in the interior is all right, in the same city it's too near, embarrassing in front of relatives. I said hey-yee! Old Mistress, you don't know these old business families in the Old City; they keep to themselves, ordinarily they'd never give their daughters to outsiders —isn't that so?'

Bingfa's wife said uncertainly, 'Of course nothing could be better if she's to go over there as the big one.'

'I don't blame you for being uneasy, but go outside and ask around: Does a family like theirs have to cheat to get a concubine? It was all because of what Old Mistress said before, as the second branch has no wife the concubine will have to run the house, so she has to be from a respectable family and can read and write and calculate, on top of being pretty. That made it difficult, otherwise they wouldn't have put it off for so long—lucky for your young miss. You wait and see: the three teas, the six gifts, the red lamps, the flowered sedan-chair, all the usual marriage trimmings, if there's one thing missing, just collar Old Wu and slap her face. Really when good luck comes, even the city wall can't hold it back. I don't know what good deeds your ancestors must have done. You can't find such a match even if you go looking for it with a lantern.'

Bingfa cleared his throat. 'Aunt Wu is no outsider, it's all right to tell you, we'd want to ask my sister first——'

'After all a brother and sister-in-law are not the same as parents,' his wife put in. 'This is a matter of a lifetime. Best to ask herself.'

'Sure, ask her. Your young miss is no fool. Their two young mistresses, one is a daughter of the Mas of Kaifeng, the other is Premier Wu's granddaughter, and both beauties, the pick of the pick. Their Second Master is just three years older than your young lady. His eyes are inconvenient but everybody says he's the best of the brothers. So learned and as gentle as a girl. In case your young lady goes over there and finds any one thing I said to be untrue, if she tells me to die standing up I won't dare die sitting down.'

They all laughed. She left saying she would come for the answer tomorrow. After a whispered consultation Bingfa's wife went into Yindi's room. She was sewing with her back to the door.

'Miss, you must have heard what Aunt Wu said.' But she sat down and told her everything all over again. 'What do you think, Miss?' she asked several times without getting an answer but no tears either, which emboldened her to snatch the sewing away. 'Talk, Miss.'

Yindi kept her head down and started to pluck veins off her palm-leaf fan.

'Speak, Miss.'

Finally, with a violent twist of her body that sent the long pigtail flying into the air, she turned around in her chair to face the other way. 'Such a nuisance!'

'At last Miss has opened her golden mouth.'

Bingfa's wife got up and did obeisance half-laughing, placing one hand on top of the other over her right ribs and moving the hands up and down a bit. 'So then congratulations, Miss.'

She was gone. The room seemed changed and the lamp-light had taken on a reddish tint. Yindi sat plucking veins off her fan. So the man she married would never see what she looked like. Part of her died at this. All the blind men she knew told fortunes. Some had horrible-looking eyes. What kind did he have? You must not believe match-makers. What else was wrong? It must be something very bad. But amidst the sense of danger and treachery she already saw him as the young Peking opera actor in a night scene sitting with an elbow on the table, eyes closed on the handsome face painted pink and white. It was as if she was to live out the rest of her life on a lighted stage with music accompanying her every movement. Or on a lighted lantern like the painted figures on it, their red sleeves turned a pale orange against the light.

She thought of Young Liu. It was all his own fault for not sending the matchmaker earlier. That was just like him. People like that would never amount to much in the world. For all you know he had hesitated because people talked about her. She felt sorry about it all the same. But wasn't it fate that he should wait until the same day as the Yaos?

The sound of the neighbours' babies crying, the angry

21

voices and loud spitting, the scuffling of a slipper sole rubbing out the spit on the floorboards, these familiar night noises seemed to be already receding into the distance. How tired she was of being poor. Every little thing could become a sin or sacrifice and turn people against each other. She had known that ever since her mother died. When her father died she was still little and her brother was not yet married. If only her mother was here to hear the news.

Her straw mat rustled and crunched all night with her turning and tossing. The cocks were crowing when she went to sleep. Soon she was awakened by the night-soil cart coming from afar in the moist grey dawn, the wooden wheels rattling over the cobblestones. Every now and then one of the men pushing and pulling it gave a yell to wake up everybody to come out and empty their chamber pots. The cry heard in half-sleep sounded even louder and more terrifying, a short gruff bark with no word to it, curiously uncertain as if he was the only man in the world and no longer knew how to speak, ecstatic too because it was all his, all the desolation.

Her sister-in-law was up. It was not a girl's place to go out groping in the dark. The thumps of the bound feet on the stairs were as heavy and well-spaced as a gang of labourers beating down piling. After a while a board rattled as it was forced down from the shopfront. She dozed off again in these every-day noises, reassuringly close.

3

Even before the wedding the Chais had started making preparations for the 'third day's homecoming'. The shop was boarded up with only one panel left out to make a narrow entrance. Written on a slip of red paper pasted across the boards were two lines, *Joyful event in the family. Business suspended for the day.*

Everything was ready. A sacrificial table was set up in the rear of the shop hung with second-hand ancestral portraits. Bingfa had chosen plump personable men and women in court gowns of lower ranks. Government posts being openly on sale nowadays, anybody fairly well off would buy himself at least a title. The embroidered chair covers and apron for the table were rented but the table-ware and candlesticks and incense pot were all newly bought with a grim kind of enjoyment. There are occasions in life when extravagances become necessities and one can indulge with a clear conscience.

Relatives had already arrived when Aunt Wu came with the news that the bride and groom would not be coming. Second Master was not well and Old Mistress did not think he should risk going out. He had always been delicate. Bingfa and his wife gathered that he wanted to get out of kotowing to the Chais' ancestors or maybe Old Mistress did not want him to. Everybody asked after him but obviously all thought it was just an excuse.

Aunt Wu had refused to come today because she insisted that she could not sit with Second Master and his bride. But now there was no reason why she should not stay for dinner. Bingfa and his wife had to swallow their anger,

23

mostly directed against her, the matchmaker, and drag her to the feast.

The dinner was ordered from a restaurant. The hors-d'oeuvres had already been set out for a long time on the sacrificial table for the enjoyment of the spirits and the flies. The dishes were now brought over to the dinner table. Aunt Wu left as soon as the meal was over, to give the Chais no chance to complain to her in private. The others were still sitting around talking when they heard children shouting in the street, 'See the bride! See the bride!'

'Not ours?' they said.

The bearers of square cakes were already at the door. The shocking-pink cakes stacked in tall cupboards that dangled from shoulder poles always heralded the bride coming home. The Chais rushed to set off the firecrackers exactly when the sedan-chairs arrived, put away the chairs and the round table-top to make room, and tip and direct the bearers to the rear. The two closed chairs of bright green felt were followed on foot by servants and two joy matrons, the professional bridesmaids. Servants lifted the groom out and carried him on a man's back. Another walking close beside him pushed his black satin cap back when it was about to fall off. Bingfa saw for the first time the man his sister had married, hunch-backed and pigeon-breasted, panting as if he had asthma. The pale clean-cut face seemed too large for the bunched-up frame. The eyes were not too noticeable, tilted slits now closed, now squinting upward, empty. Stunned at first, Bingfa helped the Yao servants drive the spectators away, stretching out his arms smiling, saying, 'Sorry, sorry, everybody make room. It's just the family today.'

Everybody smiled back not looking at him and stood their ground on tiptoes. Quite a crowd had gathered in

24

no time. Next came the bride held up at the elbows by two joy matrons. Her elaborate pearl cap covered the hair completely, making a pointed arch low on the forehead like the cut of the bangs. The encrusted head flashed white in the sun. The eyes looked down under the overhanging pearl tassels and pearl flowers, the rouged eyelid all one piece with the deep pink cheek. She wore a dark blue loose jacket and scarlet pleated skirt. A sash hung down in each narrow pleat, dangling a little gold bell, the tinkle drowned by the firecrackers.

The man hired to help out had already put up the last board but the people still hung around the shopfront, the women holding their babies. Some of the bigger boys grumbled, 'What's so rare that we're not allowed to see? Want to put him in a tent at the City God's Temple and charge three coppers for a peep?'

'Three coppers for a peep, three coppers for a peep!' the children jumped up and down singing. The servants chased them away and they came back again and stood off at the corner chanting, leaping up and down.

After the ceremony another table was laid with the newly-weds in the seats of honour facing outwards. The groom could not sit up straight. He slid far down, the bride seemed very tall beside him, long in the torso, the way idols sat. It was dark in there except for the pair of big red candles on the sacrificial table behind them. The other guests made conversation with the hostess and the joy matrons.

'Have tea, *Gu Ya* and *Gu Nana*,' Bingfa's wife used the polite terms for the son-in-law and the married daughter of the house, called Master of Miss and Madame Miss. She offered them tea with a green olive on the lid of the cup and quoted the well-wishing phrase that puns on *ching guo*, green olive, '*Ching ching jurh jurh*, billing and cooing.'

The joy matrons took it up from there. Both petite, in their thirties, dressed in dark clothes, one of them reached for some sugared dates and set them before the newlyweds. 'Bride and groom, have some *mi tzao*,' she chirped. '*Tien tien mi mi!* So sweet on each other!'

The other offered them balls of parched rice. 'Bride and groom, eat up this *huan-hsi tuan*. *Tuan tuan yuen yuen*, always together.'

Her companion set down a handful of red dates and dragon eyes. 'Bride, have some *dzao dze* and *gwei yuen*. *Dzao sheng gwei dze*, give birth soon to a son who will be a high official.'

They rattled off the phrases one after the other while the couple sat idol-like leaving their offerings untouched.

Bingfa's wife whispered, 'Does *Gu Nana* wish to go upstairs and rest a while?' It was expected of the bride that she would want to be alone with the women of her own family and have a good cry.

She got up and they went upstairs together. Her old room was empty. The bed stripped of bed-curtains had nothing on it but an old mat. The chair had been taken downstairs where it was needed with all the people coming. Dust had settled on the bare table. She felt as if she had died and was back as a ghost.

'Come to my room, *Gu Nana*. There's nowhere to sit here.'

But she went in and sat down on the bed. Bingfa's wife sat down beside her. She began to cry. For a while her sister-in-law did not know what to say.

'Don't feel bad, *Gu Nana*. *Gu Ya's* health is poor but it's not as if he has to go out and earn a living. What is there to worry about in a family like theirs? He depends on you for everything, and that's more than most married couples can say. *Gu Nana* has always wanted to be the

26

best. So many people envy you now. You'd be a fool not to know.'

She turned away.

'Don't feel bad, *Gu Nana*, in a year or so you'll have a son. With his opportunities there's no telling what he will get to be. Your later years will be your best yet.'

The rouge rubbed off Yindi's wet cheeks stained her handkerchief pink.

'Don't feel bad, *Gu Nana*, you'll ruin your make-up. Let me go and get you a hot towel.' But there was a sudden hubbub downstairs. It seemed to come from outside. She went and looked out of the window.

It was the sedan-chair carriers arguing over their tips couching it in the most auspicious phrasing, 'Rise in officialdom, Master-in-law! Rise higher!' they clamoured.

Somebody came running upstairs, her eldest boy. 'Father says to get him some more money,' he whispered and waited at the door.

'All right, I'll be right down.' She in turn waited for him to go down before she went to open the trunk in her room.

Yindi took a peep standing well to one side of the window. The thick crowd looked black at the door. The grey cobblestones were spattered with bits of pinkish red paper from the firecrackers. A ladder leaned against the wall a few feet away had a man's shirt knotted on one of the rungs. She recognized the willow-striped cotton. It was that carpenter's ladder—back from a job of work just in time to watch the fun. There was Young Liu across the street, the face leaping to the eye making the rest of them just a humming blur. He stood outside with another clerk, both looking this way with hands folded at their back, smiling slightly like everybody else. All those pairs of dark glistening eyes like flies settled on an open wound. She had known it was going to be bad but there had seemed no choice but to stick it out. In fact she was furious when she heard that this visit had been cancelled. It had been such a quiet wedding. The betrothal gifts were just simple gold and silver jewellery, six of each, northern custom her brother had said. The trousseau that the Yaos had offered to buy for her with a great show of understanding, first sent to her home, then paraded to their house—the passage of the trousseau—made a poor show. The attitudes of the servants and relatives were plain to see. What kind of a marriage was this if there weren't even any third day's homecoming? How was she going to live among them? She could not let it pass.

She had not said a single word to the bridegroom ever since she came. But this morning when she learned for sure that they were not going she had broken her silence to tell him how his family must look down on her.

'Come sit over here; I can't hear you,' he had said looking disgustingly happy.

'Are you deaf as well as blind?'

She found him more tolerable when he lapsed back into his usual sullenness, his face blank and closed. She came and sat beside him on the bed. For a while neither of them spoke. She lifted a corner of the large silk handkerchief tucked under a button and dabbed daintily at her lips with it. She glanced at him sideways and flicked his face with the handkerchief. 'Angry?'

'Angry? What about?' His hand found her knee and slowly crept upwards.

'No, don't. Don't. "In bed, husband and wife; out of bed, lady and gentleman." Somebody may come in any minute and how am I going to live this down? You don't care. Don't—listen! If you don't go home with me today and kotow to my parents you're not their son-in-law and

28

I'll never have anything to do with you again. See if I don't mean it.'

'It's not me that said anything about not going.'

But she knew he did not like to go out and a shop was after all not like a private house. 'Then speak to Old Mistress.'

'Who ever heard of a bridegroom of two days speaking for the bride? Embarrassing.'

'You embarrassed? You're shameless.' She pushed him away and quickly buttoned up her jacket looking around the bed-curtains to see if anyone was coming. His face stiffened. To soften the blow she added, 'Men are all like this,' and gave him another push.

He melted at once. 'Don't worry, I'll do what I can,' he finally said. 'I know, it's all because of your filial piety.'

Putting it all on filial piety, the highest virtue, so he need not feel ashamed for giving in to her. So here they were, trapped across the border in the land of the living, smaller than she remembered but still the only real world with people she knew, and she could kill them all looking down from her window.

The hubbub had grown louder after Bingfa's wife went down and he had presumably passed around the new batch of tips.

'Rise higher, Master-in-law!'

'All right, all right, you people, level your heart a bit,' the Yao servants intervening added to the noise. The sedan-chairs, no longer used except on occasions like these, had been hired along with the bearers. 'Master-in-law is being polite to you, and still so greedy?' said the servants of the house. 'That's enough, Master-in-law has granted face, so all right now. See if we don't tell on you when we get back.'

'Rise higher, Master-in-law, rise higher!'

29

4

Old Hsia's wide empty sleeves hung down by her sides. Her arms had managed to wriggle into the body of her roomy padded jacket to hug herself across the bosom, a favourite trick of hers in winter-time. It was cold in the vast cellar-like kitchen under the murky electric light. The dawn outside the small barred window was the greyish-green colour of crabs. A cock was crowing in the backyard, astonishingly loud and near, the long wavering croak like a cracked bamboo pole shakily extended skywards.

The cook had gone marketing. 'Second knife,' the cook's helper, and another man who did odd jobs around the kitchen were shuffling about the backyard gargling, yawning, spitting, coughing, rinsing rice under the spluttering faucet. Every one of these early morning sounds gave old Hsia a not unpleasant shiver.

She had been with the Yaos many years, drifting from post to post, unwanted because of her fondness for garlic and later because she had gone almost completely bald. She pinned on a false bun no bigger than a silver Mexican dollar and not much thicker. The glistening pate she painted with soot in a manner that was more stylized than realistic. Now though she had found a place with Second Master's bride. The new Second Mistress was entitled to four amahs and two slave girls like the other young mistresses, so she had been assigned to her just to make up the right number.

A girl in a pink padded jacket and russet silk trousers came into the kitchen rubbing her eyes, her pigtail fuzzed with sleep. 'Morning, Mistress Hsia,' she said. She put out a hand to feel one of the kettles caked with black soot sitting on the whitewashed mud stove. The water was not hot. She grimaced when she saw her stained fingers and tried to wipe them on Old Hsia's head.

'What are you doing, you little devil?' Old Hsia cried shying away from her.

'Let me smear it on for you.'

'Stop it, Lahmei.'

Lahmei looked down at her fingers and found that they were even blacker than before. 'So you've done your hair already,' she grumbled wiping her hand on the cook's soiled blue apron hanging on a nail on the wall. 'That's why you came down so early. So nobody will see you putting on your hair.'

'Don't talk nonsense. If I come down late I won't be able to get any hot water. Every morning there's a fight over the water. I'd be waiting for ages for a kettle to boil and somebody would snatch it right under my nose.'

Lahmei pushed back her sleeves reaching across the stove to feel another kettle. 'What's the matter with this one?' she said as she lifted it off the fire. 'It's warm enough.'

'Hey, that's mine! There is such a thing as first come, first served.'

'Big Mistress is waiting to wash her face. She'll scold if I'm late.'

'Second Mistress will also scold.'

'She can't, she's still practically a bride.'

'Huh! You just haven't heard her.'

'How? What does she say?' Lahmei whispered leaning over, interested at once. Old Hsia tried to wrest the kettle from her.

'Give it back quick.'

'I wonder where Cook is getting our oil now. Won't Second Mistress be offended if we buy it elsewhere?'

'That will do from you. Now give it back.'

'See? Spill it all and there's none for anybody. Why don't you take that one over there, it's humming already.'

'I don't hear anything.'

'You must be getting stone deaf, Mistress Hsia.'

After the girl had gone off with the kettle Old Hsia found that she had been deceived. The other kettle was only luke-warm. Muttering she resigned herself to another long wait. But more people were coming in. She had better take it upstairs before they could lay hands on it. It would have to do.

The light was on in every room. There was a lot of muffled activity with amahs and slave girls scurrying about. The daughters-in-law were getting ready to go and wish Old Mistress good morning. She was an early riser.

'I thought you'd dropped dead downstairs,' Yindi turned around and whispered between her teeth. The hair-dresser-amah was putting finishing touches to her hair. The bangs were pushed up with a small ivory comb because she had not yet washed her face.

'I waited and waited but somebody always comes along and grabs it. This time it was Big Mistress's Lahmei. Like robbers every one of them.'

'Why do you let them? Are you dead?' Her voice rose although Second Master was still sleeping. A pair of large silver hooks hung motionless outside the closed bed-curtains of pale turquoise silk.

Old Hsia said nothing. But turning around to pour water into the enamel basin on the rosewood stand with her back to Yindi her lips moved strenuously in the set face framing a silent stream of protests. All this talk of 'Are you dead?' and 'Thought you'd dropped dead' was especially unhealthy first thing in the morning. And all in front of the hairdresser-amah who was much behind her

32

in seniority. Call it bad luck to be working for this branch, put into situations like these. It's difficult for servants and the others are dogs presuming on the owners' power. Let her go down herself next time and see for herself how it is.

'Rice pot, good for nothing but to hold rice,' Yindi muttered going to the wash-stand. Old Hsia expected another explosion when she found out how cold the water was but she was in too much of a hurry. All she did was wipe the corners of the eyes, then mix some face powder with water cupped in her palm and smear it on. She tore off a piece of crimson cotton wool, dipped it in the basin and rubbed it on her lower lip making a perfectly round red spot, the current abstract representation of the small cherry mouth. She had noticed that the women of the house used much more rouge than was customary and there were heavily painted middle-aged women among their relatives. They were northerners, countrified by Shanghai standards. Their clothes also—all the fashionable pale colours were forbidden—too like light mourning. Old Mistress would say, 'I'm not dead yet, no need to wear mourning.' Pale cheeks were also called funereal. Yindi steeled herself to smear both palms red and simply draw them down the sides of her face from eyelids down.

She was helped out of her overall cape. The two little slave girls were waiting with her rings and gold nail sheaths for the two little fingers where she had let the nails grow. The hairdresser helped to straighten her tight fur-lined jacket with a tug from behind as she hurried from the room.

She was late again. There was no one in the anteroom where they waited for their mother-in-law to wake up. Through the half-closed door and scarlet felt curtain she could hear Old Mistress loudly, gratingly clearing her throat in two syllables with the accent on the second, khum *khum*! Her wooden platform soles hit the floor as she got up, a flat hard thump. Being very small she always sat with her feet off the ground.

It was one of her pet notions to hang a red dishcloth of feather-patterned gauze on the brass door knob to wrap it around the polished handle every time the door was opened or closed, so it would not be tarnished by hands touching it. Yindi realized that she had forgotten to make use of the cloth when she saw Old Mistress look at her oddly.

'Mother,' she murmured.

Old Mistress acknowledged the greeting with a faraway 'Hm' at the back of the nose. She sucked at her long pipe, her sharp chin curling out from the little walnut face. She turned to her right and aimed the chin at Big Mistress. 'We must seem like country bumpkins, getting up at dawn.'

Big Mistress and Third Mistress smiled discreetly into their handkerchiefs.

She directed her chin at Third Mistress. 'We're behind the times. Nowadays people no longer have shame, nothing like before.'

Nobody dared smile any more. Late rising could only mean one thing, especially with newly-weds. In her case with the bridegroom in such poor health, the bride must be really rapacious and inconsiderate. Yindi's colour drained away instantly leaving the rouge stranded on her face like the crimson patches on a green apple. Old Mistress scarcely ever spoke to her as a rule except to ask about Second Master's health. But she seemed to want to make things easier for her, telling the others, 'Second Mistress is new here, she doesn't know our ways. She's a southerner, their customs are different,' when the real difference between her world and theirs was not

34

geographical. Now she knew her period of immunity as a bride was over.

The large whitewashed room was well-ventilated, chilly with just a brass brazier on a low claw-footed wooden tripod painted scarlet and gold.

'Shut that window, the wind has shifted,' Old Mistress told a slave girl. She was a weather station in herself. 'Open this one part way. The top pane, you fool, look at that draught. Go and rub that door knob. It's impossible to keep it bright with people pawing it all the time.' She knocked out the ashes of her pipe on the rosewood couch. 'The winters here are not so bad compared to Nanking. Of course there the brick floor made a difference. Huh! you should have seen the main bedroom —a whole row of paving bricks caved in where the daughters-in-law stood at attention all day. You people don't know how well off you are.'

The children of the eldest branch came in to greet their grandmother, hanging back near the door with their own amahs behind them just outside ready to answer any questions from Old Mistress. After them came the old concubines. Next to put in an appearance was the eldest son. Yindi murmured 'Big Master' together with Third Mistress. He answered 'Ai' quickly with a half startled air as if he had not known they were here, bobbing his head vaguely in their direction without looking, as was proper. He sat down while they remained standing. He was tall and thin with large eyes and a bony well-cut face. Old Mistress asked him about tonight's dinner party and a letter from the keeper of the ancestral graves. Soon he mumbled something about an appointment and got away.

At about eleven o'clock Old Mistress asked, 'Third Master not up yet?'

'I don't know, I'll tell them to go and see.' Third

35

Mistress went to speak to one of her amahs waiting outside the door but Old Mistress stopped her.

'Let him sleep. He came back late again didn't he?' she said accusingly.

'No, he was early last night but I heard him coughing. It may have kept him awake.'

'It's the weather. I have a cough coming on too,' Old Mistress said.

'Will you have some almond milk, Mother? It may help,' Big Mistress said. 'We'll make it ourselves. The servants' hands aren't clean.'

Old Mistress nodded. 'How is Second Master?' she turned to Yindi. 'How is his asthma?'

Reprieve. She had been spoken to.

'Second Master is better today. He says the new prescription seems to help.' She had to be careful not to sound hoarse; her voice had not been used for so long. She stood at ease, back in the world again.

Old Mistress set the slave girls to cut rings out of red paper and loop them around narcissus stems. The daughters-in-law joined in the work. The plants had been bought for the New Year, set in rows in porcelain bowls, shallow rectangles filled with pebbles and water. The yellow-centred white blossoms were considered too funereal for the New Year, a dash of red had to be added for luck.

She had sent the carriage for a grand-niece. Lunch was served in the bedroom. Ordinarily she ate alone with the daughters-in-law in attendance but she made them eat with her today to keep the little guest company. The dishes rested on fluted tin bowls filled with hot water, except for the chicken which was in a big earthen pot. Yindi had learned to be wary of the soup which looked deceptively cool, the steam being sealed off by the thick film of yellow grease broken only by the drumsticks that stuck out like tilted masts. Old Mistress liked her food scalding hot.

'Huh! this chicken is older than I, the Old Mistress,' she said chewing. 'The addled egg of a cook is padding his accounts. The incestuous turtle egg. Lain by a dog.' She swore like a mandarin, having been a widow and head of the house so long she had become mannish. Yindi had never heard anything like it. She took a spoonful of soup. 'Huh! this chicken is even saltier than I, the Old Mistress.'

She cursed so much she slipped. The daughters-in-law looked down into their own rice bowls. It was always safer not to smile. The thin chain connecting a pair of silver chopsticks tinkled in the silence.

After she had lain down for her afternoon nap they retired to the anteroom and sat around a table peeling almonds which had been soaked first in hot water. Their hands were pale against the scarlet rug spread over the table.

'Let's play mahjong,' Big Mistress whispered giggling. 'Spread another blanket over the table and you can't hear from the next room.'

'There's only three of us,' Third Mistress said.

'Wait till Third Master gets up,' Yindi said.

'Third Master will never play for such small stakes.' Big Mistress crossed her legs and looked rather doubtfully at her new shoes of black gauze open-work over pink satin with a foreign word cut out. 'I wonder what it means,' she said to Third Mistress. 'I asked your Third Master to write me a foreign word when I was making these shoes. When Big Master saw them he said it says "*horse hoof*. And that's the fitting word for you."'

Everybody laughed. The stunted bound feet could be hoof-like.

'Big Master was teasing you,' said Third Mistress.

'I don't know. It's just like Third Master to think of a thing like that.'

'He's capable of anything,' his wife agreed.

Both the brothers learned English as a bypath to officialdom. Boys who did not do well at classical studies and had no hope of passing the imperial examinations were usually set to study foreign affairs. The Yaos had a resident foreign tutor guaranteed to be a real Englishman. He lived by himself in a three-storey house in the garden. The brothers were supposed to go to him bringing him questions on *sheng, guang, hua, dien,* sound, light, chemistry, electricity, generally conceded to be foreigners' special province. The teacher had to stay in waiting for them although they seldom ever came. When they did come they had fun teaching the tutor to swear in Chinese. Once a year on the ninth of the ninth moon when it's good luck to go up a hill or any high place, the Englishman was asked beforehand to vacate the premises so the ladies could come to his house and climb up to the third storey. It was the highest building for miles around and commanded a pretty view. They could see the Bund, the Race Course and the fashionable Chang Park.

'Why don't you trace the word on a piece of paper and have somebody take it to the foreign teacher and ask him?' Yindi said.

'You can't do that,' Big Mistress said, blushing a little. 'Who knows what it says? Maybe worse than horse hoof.'

Yindi said giggling, 'I know. Just wait till the foreigner is out walking in the garden and you walk past him in these shoes. If he laughs it must be horse hoof.'

The other two had a look of constraint on their faces although they joked constantly among themselves. She examined her nails, they ached and felt stuffed from peeling almonds. She purposely rinsed her fingers

38

sacrilegiously in the water soaking the nuts, got up and looked out of the window. They lived in what was called a merry-go-round building with a small courtyard in the centre of the house. The upstairs windows looked down into the dark stone-paved square as into a well. There was nothing to see but it happened that she had not stood there for long when a private ricksha came out of the corridor walk and parked in the courtyard.

'Look who's here!' He looked like his big brother actually except that his eyebrows and eyelashes were thicker and his hair grew low. Even shaved to make a high forehead there was the green shadow of a widow's peak. 'Why I thought Third Master is still in bed. How is it he's just back?'

'Oh?' Third Mistress said vaguely. 'He must have slipped out then.'

'See what a model wife she is,' Yindi said to Big Mistress, 'telling lies to shield her husband.'

'Who's shielding him? How was I to know if he was out or not? I've been with you people all the time.'

'All right, all right, we're all with you,' Yindi said. 'If Old Mistress gets angry everybody is done for.'

The young man who stepped off the ricksha had disappeared into one of the rooms behind the porch. A feather duster dyed bright pink and green was stuck at the back of the seat like a tail held high. The ricksha-puller took it down and started to dust the new vehicle with obvious pride and pleasure. It had four acetylene lanterns, called water-moon lamps because of the bluish white brilliance. Third Master liked to ride around at night illuminated from top to toe like a singsong girl answering summonses to dinner parties.

'We must tell Third Master what a good wife he has, and he's so ungrateful, running out day and night.'

Third Mistress didn't say anything, so Big Mistress came to her rescue. 'Big Master is just as bad. Who's like Second Master, staying home all the time to keep you company?'

'Yes, we've always said you're better off than any of us, Second Sister-in-law', Third Mistress chimed in. 'Really husbands as good as Second Master are hard to find.'

Yindi had turned back to the window. Third Master's ricksha-puller was sitting on the foot perch puffing at his pipe, pulling up his long white cloth socks.

'Looks like he's going out again any minute,' she said.

'What took so long at the book-keeper's office?' she said.

Her sisters-in-law went on talking about clothes for the New Year. They knew why as well as she did. Everybody needs money for the New Year.

A manservant crossed the courtyard bearing a large wooden tray laden with dishes and a rice pot heading for the book-keeper's room.

'Lunch, this late? Or is it breakfast? For two,' she observed the two pairs of chopsticks.

Next came a basin of hot water for the diners to wash their faces. Another man fetched the spare box of combs that Third Master kept in his study. He seemed to want his pigtail rebraided.

'He might as well move in with the book-keeper,' she giggled. 'Really, with our Third Master it's "Whoever has milk is Mother." '

An amah came in and said to Third Mistress, 'Miss, Third Master wants his sable-lined gown.' Old Li had come with Third Mistress from her maiden home as a 'room companion', a useful institution designed to make things easier for the young bride suddenly uprooted and dropped into the midst of hostile in-laws. Every time she called her Miss it reminded Yindi that she herself had not brought any.

'Oh, is he upstairs?' Third Mistress felt for the bunch of keys that dangled from the button under her arm.

'No, he sent a man up.' The exchange was in semi-private whispers.

'Don't get it for him, Third Mistress,' Yindi said loudly with mock authority. 'Never home except for a change of clothes, and off again he goes.'

'Well, if it's all right with Third Mistress, we shouldn't be busybodies,' Big Mistress said half laughing.

'I'll be a busybody just for this once. I can't stand the way he bullies your young lady, Old Li. Go and tell him to come and get it himself.'

Old Li smiled but made no move to leave the room. Third Mistress also smiled as she searched among her keys.

'Don't let him have it, Third Mistress. Why are you so afraid of him?'

'Who's afraid of him? Only I'd just as soon he goes out, more peace and quiet. We're not such a loving couple as you and Second Master.'

'Us! a good thing you're not like us.'

'It's just that I don't want to quarrel with him. Old Mistress will say I'm driving him away from home.'

'Yes, the woman always gets the blame,' Yindi said. 'You'll be blamed too if Old Mistress finds out you've been covering up for him.' And Third Mistress felt sickeningly certain that she would hear of it soon. 'She'd say that you let him do whatever he likes just to please him.'

'Yes, it's always the wife's fault,' said Third Mistress.

'Old Li, go tell Third Master that Old Mistress asked for him,' Yindi said half laughing. 'We're all in for it when it gets known that he's gone without coming in.'

Old Li looked at Third Mistress, who dropped her eyes and jerked her head slightly towards the door. Old Li went.

41

5

It was dark in the book-keeper's office. The old rattan chairs had turned a greasy dark yellow, each with a round hole on the right arm to hold a teacup. A servant brought in a black kettle to add water to the tea. Third Master had taken the rattan chaise-longue but he sat leaning forward smiling at the book-keeper with a mock-earnest look, holding his own hand with elbows resting on parted knees. The deerskin sleeveless jacket he wore over his gown was buttoned across the chest with heavy black satin trimming. The latest hair style for men was 'a sky full of stars', a short fringe over the artificial high round forehead called 'the moon gate', brought in by the Manchus. As the upper part of the physiognomy corresponds to heaven and the lower part to earth, all these names were astronomically inspired. The fringe was so short it stuck straight out, mere dots seen from the front, therefore likened to countless stars. The curious combined effect of a receding hairline with projecting bangs did not look bad on him. That's the thing about fashion.

'All right, all right, Old Mr Chu, now don't be difficult,' he said.

Old Mr Chu shook his head picking his teeth with a bit of rattan broken off the chair arm. 'Third Master is making it very awkward for me. Nobody is to draw money from now on without asking for permission. Old Mistress has spoken.'

'Lend a hand, lend a hand. Just this once. It won't set a precedent.'

'If only it's up to me, Third Master.'

'Come on, spread it under some other items—as if I have to teach you your trade.'

42

'I've taken a lot of risks for Third Master, by heaven and earth and conscience. This time I really don't know what to do.'

'Then raise some money for me. You're a rich man yourself.'

The old man became agitated. 'Where did Third Master hear this? Where would I have got money after thirty years in your house?'

'Who knows? Maybe your wife has been making money for you all these years you've been away.'

'This Third Master is always like this!' The old man laughed at the familiar joke.

'Anyway everybody knows you have money, no use denying.'

'The bit of coffin money I saved up is not enough to fill the space between Third Master's teeth.'

'You'll have to do me this favour today no matter what. I leave it in your hands.' He did obeisance without bothering to get up, right hand over left fist, jerking them up and down repeatedly with little bows.

'Money is tight at the end of the year,' Old Mr Chu ruminated and clucked regretfully. 'Unless we go to that Shansi man. Wonder if he has that much at hand.'

'Go and see, quick.' He took Old Chu's black satin skull-cap from where it had been sitting on top of the hat vase, a cylinder of pale blue crackle-china, and slapped it on his head.

'These Moslems from Shansi, they're hard. You happen to go to one of them, then there's nothing to say, he has to have his three tenths.'

'No matter what he wants, I don't want it if the money is not here today.'

'Third Master is always in such a hurry, as if his eyebrows are on fire.'

'Go quick. I'll take a nap in your room, played mahjong all night last night.'

'Aren't you going upstairs? Just now they said Old Mistress wants you.'

'Tell them I'm gone. Once Old Mistress gets hold of me I won't be able to go out again.' On second thought he said, 'All right, I'll wait for you upstairs.' With him in the room Old Chu would not be able to open his trunk and get out his passbook and go to the money shop. Of course there wasn't any Moslem from Shansi. It's easier to talk terms by inventing a third party. Easier also to get the money back. He knew something about loans.

He came upstairs. The three women were peeling almonds in the anteroom.

'Big Sister-in-law, Second Sister-in-law,' he mumbled as he pulled a chair around, neatly flipped up the back hem of his gown, sat down astride the chair and started to pop almonds into his mouth.

'Look at him,' Yindi said. 'Here we've been slaving at it all afternoon and he comes and eats it all up.'

He said, 'Who faked the imperial dispatch? Isn't Old Mistress having her nap?'

'She'll wake up soon,' Third Mistress said.

'Third Master, what's that word you wrote for my shoes?' said Big Mistress.

'What word?'

'The foreign word. So you bully people who don't know the language, call them names. Horse hoofs.'

He could not help letting out a chuckle at which she cried out, 'It's wicked. Ruin people's shoes for no reason.'

'Isn't that so?' said Third Mistress. 'This cut-out pattern is such a lot of work too. But it seems to be the only thing this year.'

'Lucky I didn't wear it to go out.' She got up and left the room.

'Went to change shoes,' Yindi whispered.

'Had them on?' He started to laugh.

'Laughing yet,' his wife said.

He turned on her. 'Where's my fur-lined gown?'

'Now don't fly at her,' Yindi broke in. 'Your good wife was going to get it for you. It's me who played the villain, I wouldn't let her. I said don't let him have it—came home just to change clothes and go out again.'

'But Second Sister-in-law, won't your heart ache if I die of cold?' he said.

'There's the one who'll ache,' she leaned over and gave Third Mistress a little push.

'Who's like this? Unless it's you and Second Master,' Third Mistress said.

'Well, you don't see me telling lies all round for Second Master's sake and shouldering all the blame. Really, Third Master, you don't know what a model wife you have.'

Third Mistress moved the bowl out of his reach. 'All right, leave some for the almond milk for Old Mistress.'

'What's so good about it, so tasteless,' Yindi said. He got up and scooped more out of the bowl. 'Hey, look! Third Mistress, isn't it about time you put your foot down.'

'No use her putting her foot down, only Second Sister-in-law can do it,' he said.

'Listen to him, Third Mistress!' She made as if to strike him, gave Third Mistress another push instead and fell on her neck laughing. She played restlessly with the gold toothpick and ear-spoon that dangled from the other woman's lapel button and squeezed her thin shoulders as if she would like to knead her out of shape. Third Mistress had had enough of it. She got up and wiped her fingers.

45

'If you want the trunks opened it had better be before Old Mistress wakes up,' she said not looking at him. 'Come see for yourself. Who knows what you want, long-haired sable or short-haired sable.' She went out of the room.

'—Calling you,' Yindi said.

He did not say anything. He put out a hand to move the red paper ring up and down a narcissus stalk. Under his wet-looking greenish eyebrows and thick lashes the eyes were like the under-water black pebbles in the bowl of flowers.

'Where's my nail sheath?' she exclaimed half to herself. 'I had it on just now.'

'You must have dropped it when you were hitting at people. That would teach you,' he said.

'Give it back quick, or I'd really beat you.'

'Still want to hit people?'

She raised her hand. 'Are you going to give it back or no?'

'You'd better really hit me for once.' He tilted a shoulder towards her. 'This feels itchy all over.'

'Hand it over quick.'

'Sing a song and you can have it back.'

'I can't sing.'

'Wasn't it you that day humming and chirping by yourself on the veranda?'

'No such thing.'

'No use my asking you, my face is not big enough.'

'But I really can't.'

'Quick, sing,' he whispered, standing over her so she could sing without being overheard. The hem of his gown brushed the top of her feet, so sweetly it seemed a long while to her. The room stood around. The sun just touched a feather duster in a tall light blue crackle-china vase. Sunlight showed up the film of dust on the broad

46

shafts of dark green jade leaves in the off-white jade pot. An enamel clock ticked in its glass dome on the scroll table. The all too fleeting moment of privacy had gone to her head like wine.

'Look what I picked up, Second Sister-in-law.' He held up his little finger admiringly with her nail sheath on it. If she pounced on it she would be in his arms. The same madness had got into him, she could tell. She glared at him from the corner of her eyes, dipped her finger in the water bowl and snapped the two-inch rose-coloured fingernail at him shooting drops of water into his face.

She saw him duck and heard footsteps behind her. Big Mistress came in and he was back in his seat. She hoped her blush was not noticeable under the rouge.

'Old Mistress is not awake yet?' Big Mistress sat down.

'I think I heard her cough,' he said. 'I'll take a look.' He flipped up the back of his gown violently getting up and grabbed another handful of almonds.

'Put that down,' Big Mistress scolded. 'There really isn't much left.'

He tossed them back and popped into the inner room, the strip of scarlet felt curtain flapping high behind him.

Big Mistress eased the almonds into the mortar. 'What's this? Whose is this?' She laughed. 'What an expensive prescription, all this gold in it.'

'Oh, that's mine,' Yindi said. 'I was just wondering where my nail sheath had gone to. Must have slipped into the bowl.'

'Let's see if there's any more.' Big Mistress sifted the almonds in her hand. 'This time I'm going to keep it.'

Yindi shook the little gold tube dry and rubbed it on her handkerchief. She hadn't realized until then how much she had wanted him to keep it. In fact she had been worried that he would carelessly leave it around for people

47

to see. They could tell it was hers from the pattern of the carving. But his returning it seemed to have cancelled everything that happened this afternoon. It was mere horseplay to while away an hour of enforced idleness as he waited to go back to his favourite singsong girl of the moment. Big Mistress would not forget though. How much had she seen or heard?

Later she felt somewhat better when she heard that Third Master was not allowed to go out again that evening. Men guests were coming for dinner and Old Mistress insisted that both her sons should be in. It was mostly their grandfather's 'pupils', examinees that he had passed in imperial examinations. Some were very old. Although there would be only men, there was no question of calling in singsong girls to help entertain. But she heard there would be some Peking opera actors coming, female impersonators. While having dinner in her room she could hear the faint sound of laughter downstairs and the singing accompanied by the Huns' fiddle. They did not seem to be having such a dismal time after all.

After dinner she sat with her hands tucked under her jacket. There was no fire. Cold is bad for asthma but a fire is drying and binding, bad for the system. Old Mistress considered herself the only one in the house old enough to stand it. Old people with less fire in them are immune to heat. It was dark here too, with just a weak electric light darker still from the size of the room and the height of the ceiling. The room was like a huge brown jar of stale icy water. Movement was as strenuous as under water, with a feeling that a hand or foot would not go exactly in the direction it was meant to go. Like a dripping tap the ticking clock steadily added to the water reserve. She must get up, do something.

Second Master was lying fully clothed on the bed crosswise facing his opium tray, hands tucked in his sleeves. He had taken up opium because it eased his asthma and gave him something to do. As opium was forbidden in the house he had to smoke on the sly. Actually Old Mistress knew about it too. After his marriage he had indulged rather more, under the impression that it would give him virility. The cloth soles of his shoes stood out snow-white in the yellow-brown gloom. They stayed new because he never stepped on the floor.

She went and sat on the bed in order to whisper, 'I died laughing today. Third Master was out all night and Third Mistress said he wasn't up yet. Dived into the book-keeper's office as soon as he came in. Closeted together for hours and had lunch together. It's said that even Big Master can't get through the New Year. Old Mistress believes in Big Master, actually the two are much of a muchness. At this rate what are we going to live on?'

At first he did not say anything. 'We haven't come to that yet.'

What she hated most about him was he knew how to talk officialese, if nothing else. Of course he had very little use for money anyway; no wonder he could afford to be gentlemanly about it. Perhaps he would even prefer to have just enough so he would not have to envy his brothers so much. With all the pomp and pleasures boiling around them he and she were condemned to their hermitage.

The Huns' fiddle was playing downstairs again. Back in her old seat, her hands tucked under her jacket she stroked the squirrel lining as she would a cat. Did she really sing on the veranda or was she just humming? Funny that Third Master had happened to hear and re-membered. He remembered. Her heart suddenly swelled out big, squeezing the breath out of her. There was loud music, a multitude that sang so long it sounded like a

49

ringing in the ears. The afternoon came back, everything altogether, in the reflected light on the dark window pane she was looking at, with a ghostly scene floating on the brown glass and that singing that came out at you in a shining sheet.

Second Master was groping under his pillow and all round him. 'Where's my rosary?' Old Mistress encouraged him to study Buddhism and got famous monks and laymen to come and explain the scriptures to him. His favourite rosary was a string of hollowed peach stones carved intricately with buddhivestas crowding mountain caves and under trees.

She did not answer.

'Call Old Cheng for me.' He sounded annoyed.

'They're all having dinner downstairs.'

'Where's my rosary?'

'Isn't it lying around? It must have fallen on the floor.'

'Then pick it up. Somebody may step on it and break the beads.'

'Not everybody is blind.'

It was always like this, she would say something offensive just so that he would not speak to her any more. As usual finding him more tolerable in this state, she eventually came and knelt on the bed to help him look. It was hanging on the knob of one of the built-in little drawers where he kept his sweets. She leaned over and reached for it gently from the bottom upwards, cushioning it with the yellow silk tassel that hung from it so that the carved peach stones did not give the least crackle.

'Look under the beddings,' he said.

She slipped her other hand under the neat stack of silk-faced blankets. 'It's not here. Wait till the servants come. I'm not going to crawl under the bed looking for it.'

'They couldn't have put it away, I always have it at hand.'

50

'It must be somewhere around. It has no legs, it can't run away.'

She went to the cupboard, opened a drawer and took out a nut-cracker. She sat down at the table and cracked the peach stones open one by one.

'What are you doing?' he said nervously.

'Eating walnuts. Want some?'

He was silent.

'You don't like them without seasoning.'

The thin brown perforated shells snapped easily with the tiniest explosions.

'Tell one of the amahs to come upstairs,' he said. 'They've been gone a long time.'

'At least let people finish eating. Even thunder doesn't strike a sinner in the middle of a meal.'

He said no more. 'Old Cheng!' he suddenly shouted in a tight flat voice. 'Old Cheng! Old Hsia!'

'What's the matter with you? Getting odder and odder everyday. Stop that. I'll go and call them for you.' Her fingers were tired from working the nut-cracker. She had just been wondering how to dispose of the ones that were left. They were threaded on a strong fine greyish-green silk string which was quite undamaged. The remaining beads slipped, clattering lightly down the string as she picked it up. She saw him give a start and almost laughed aloud. Wrapping everything in her handkerchief she went out into the hallway.

There was nobody around. The large brown-lit hall had a watchful air with all the doors half open and the head of the polished staircase behind her. She unlatched a French window and stepped out on the dark veranda. There was some light from the windows. She glanced back to see if there might be anyone there. The freezing cold took your breath away but it felt good and clean. This was

51

the only place in the house where she could ever be alone for a minute. She crossed the floor boards on to the projecting part of the T-shaped veranda, paved with gravel that crunched underfoot. The silhouetted railing posts topped with round cement balls like monks' shaved heads always frightened her at night. She walked quickly up to them and bent down to feed the contents of her handkerchief carefully down the drain.

The red brick archway below stood on massive pillars, foreign-style, leading to the front door. The brightly lit area was strangely silent, the tarred road bluish, turning round here, the hedges with every leaf distinct like pale clusters of petals. You could not hear the voices and singing here, just now and then a rhythmic yell in the finger game. Still she stood there in the cold. She thought she heard some stir over at the lodge. If the party was breaking up she wanted to see them leave.

The first of the horse carriages drove up clickety-clock along the asphalt driveway. Private rickshas crowded up in what space there was in between. The guests filed out bowing and murmuring. The old men leaning on gnarled sticks were half smothered in fur-lined scarlet silk hoods with long ear-flaps. Young female impersonators held turquoise silk handkerchiefs to their pink-and-white faces hiding their smiles. They wore men's gowns and little black sleeveless jackets, satin-trimmed. She thought she heard Third Master on the stoop just out of sight. She pressed against the railing, the cement surface scratching her brocade jacket noisily.

The last of the guests were gone. 'Where's Ahfu? Tell him to get my ricksha out,' his voice said.

Men padded away shouting Ahfu in relays.

'It's too cold to go out in a ricksha, Third Master,' somebody said. 'Better take the carriage.'

'They'll take all night to get it ready. All right, tell them to hurry.'

More orders were called out in relays. Then silence. She wondered if he could have gone inside to wait but she did not hear the door.

She started to sing 'The Names of the Flowers of the Twelve Months'. If he had heard her sing it must have been this since it was the only one she knew at all well. It was difficult to sing half suffocated by the north wind. But the wind snatching the notes from her mouth emboldened her with a wild sense of irresponsibility. She sang louder. The song named each month's flower and doings, celebrating the New Year or picking tea leaves, breeding silk worms, watching the dragon boat race. Through it all the girl was waiting for her lover, trying to tell whether he was coming. There were lamp flowers—clusters of sparks on the burning wick—he would be here tonight. A lucky spider dropped on her head, he must be coming. Toss a pair of slippers on the ground and the way they fell showed he was not coming. The little tune had a twist in every note, always returning to itself. Under the cover of night and the monotony of repetition she was able to sing out evenly some passages about long nights and biting the padded blanket leaving teeth marks, hating the man for not coming. For a moment she felt enthralled by her own voice as if she were uncoiling her whole sinuous length, swimming away infinitely in the darkness above and below.

She did not hear him say to the servant. 'Funny there're street singers in this weather. A heroin addict out begging.'

He drove away when she got to the sixth moon with its lotus flowers and wearing just a scarlet silk stomacher after a bath.

53

6

It being her first child her brother's wife was asked to come and stay to look after her during the confinement. It turned out to be a boy. She was happy for the first time since she was married. As Bingfa's wife put it, '*Gu Nana*'s belly has shown them.'

Old Mistress was very pleased. At last her blessings were complete. Even her poor blind misshapen son had an heir to carry on his branch of the family. She was only a 'flowered' or 'patterned' vegetarian instead of a year-round one, abstaining from meat only on specific days. Still her cleanliness as a vegetarian forbade her to enter the maternity 'blood room'. She just stood at the door held up at the elbows by two strapping slave girls who dwarfed her, shouting at the amahs inside to open a window at a certain angle.

'There won't be a draught, it's south-west wind today and this room faces north-west. What do you feel like eating? Send word to the kitchen. But no ducks or your head will wobble like a duck's head. You can catch all sorts of sickness just now, you'll feel it when you get older.'

She thanked Bingfa's wife. 'She's lucky to have Mistress-in-law with her. Mistress-in-law must be worried about things at home but perhaps it would be possible to stay on a little longer, at least until the month is over. Don't act like a guest here. This is just like your own house. Be sure to ask for anything you need.'

The baby was carried to the door for inspection, bundled in red silk and tied up straight as a board in the style called 'candle package'. He had a touch of asthma. Old Mistress had heard that he had to have opium smoke breathed into his face for relief but she pretended not to know.

Second Master had moved downstairs. Yindi was happy to have him out of the way. The world was suddenly wider. She enjoyed showing her brother's wife everything. Her bridal rosewood bed was as big as a room, with framed embroidered pictures of the four seasonal plants across the front tipping forward. There were built-in shelves for vases, clock, tea set and knick-knacks. The tiers of tiny drawers inlaid with mother-of-pearl figures waving swords—the hundred and eight brigands—reminded her of all those little drawers at the pharmacy, especially the smell of one of the sweetmeats he kept there, plums cured by the sweet herb used to sweeten all medicines. Now she and her brother's wife talked all night and nibbled at the cakes and candies like two children. She had never dreamed she would ever be so close to her sister-in-law. She poured out all her complaints and often ended in tears. They felt safest whispering in bed inside the turquoise glass cloth curtains. Two little gold baskets with a touch of blue enamel stuffed with jasmine blossoms hung down from the top of the bed on thin gold chains. Every now and then came a whiff of the heavy cool fragrance. The little broom for sweeping the bed sheet had a crude tassel of red rags tied on its handle.

'Really no need to get up for days,' her sister-in-law said.

She got prickly heat from the yards of white cloth wound tightly around her to keep her figure. She had to sit up straight all day so as to bleed as much as possible and be rid of the unclean blood. She had a pleasant sense of anonymity as just a new mother. From the sunny street outside came the tinkle of ricksha bells, the plod-plod of horses' hoofs and faint rumble of carriage wheels. A man's high voice sang tunefully, 'Buy . . . washboards!' A rattle drum thumped idly, 'Dlung dung dung. Dlung dung dung.' It was the man who sold cosmetics, garters, spools of thread and loosely braided silk thread, announcing himself by shaking a rattle-drum, treating women as children.

The Full Month gifts for the baby were coming in, first sent to Old Mistress's room to be inspected, then brought to Yindi's room to be displayed on the dressing-table with the mirror covered by a piece of scarlet cloth. The new baby and its mother were both still weak and frail, their souls might wander in sleep and get trapped in the mirror. The gifts were gold and silver padlocks each with its own chain to be worn around the baby's neck and flat pendants of green jade shaped like padlocks. The baby might escape if not locked up and chained down to this life on earth. Some of the nearer relatives sent a red lacquered trayful of these trinkets.

Bingfa's wife got a little worried with so many valuables lying around. 'I hope the newcomer is reliable.' She was referring to the wet nurse in a less noticeable way if they should be overheard.

'She's all right,' Yindi said at once. 'Fresh from the country and frightened to death. The servants here haven't had time to teach her any tricks yet.'

The wet nurse was naturally more respectful than the others, not knowing anything about her. So she liked her, they never had any new faces in this house. Wet nurses were traditionally pampered. They got new clothes and gold jewellery and ate by themselves with special dishes to 'generate milk'. This one had enough to spare and milked herself into a cup for Old Mistress to take first thing every morning, the best tonic. Yindi had reason to be proud of her. Old Mistress could not abide cow's milk.

Big Mistress, Third Mistress and the old concubines

came in to see the presents. Another time Third Mistress showed them to visiting cousins.

'Are these from Maternal Uncle?' somebody pointed to a set of loaded trays. The maternal uncle had to give a number of gold chains and padlocks, bangles, anklets, pendants, medallions for hats, embroidered suits with hats, cloaks and shoes to match and silk blankets for all seasons.

'No, those aren't here yet,' Third Mistress mumbled looking away as if embarrassed.

Yindi got really worried after they were gone. 'Not here yet,' she whispered to Bingfa's wife.

'If it's not here by tomorrow I'll go back again and see.'

'You heard those people.'

'People are envious.'

'Of course, some have been here for years without letting out a fart, not to say a son. And their husbands aren't coffin-stuffing either.'

Third Mistress had no children.

Bingfa came the next day instead of sending the presents. Male relatives were generally not taken upstairs but this was a special occasion.

'Master-in-law brought this,' said Old Cheng behind him carrying a heavy double-decked container of bamboo strips and wood trim painted a brownish-crimson.

'Ai-ya, what ever for?' Yindi spoke from her bed. 'Really, Brother shouldn't have gone to all this trouble.'

'Let's see what you have here.' His wife lifted the lid off. There was a big plate of steamed pork wrapped in lotus leaves. The lower deck had a glazed earthen pot with a whole hen and half a ham in soup.

'Old Cheng, give some of this to the wet nurse,' Yindi said.

Bingfa wore a formal black gauze jacket over his gown

57

and sat waving a plain black fan. His wife showed him the baby.

'Everybody well at home?' she said. She waited until the amahs were gone before she asked, 'What about the Full Month gift? We're worried to death here.'

'That's why I'm desperate. I had to come and talk it over with *Gu Nana*.'

They spoke in whispers, a pause after every sentence. Sitting far apart they all bent forward to hear better, he with elbows planted on spread knees, the folded fan held in between. Nobody was fanning so as not to make the least noise.

'Sister-in-law knows I have no money,' Yindi said. 'She's seen for herself now.' But what did she see except the way they lived? Who would believe that all she got was her tiny monthly allowance, no more than a servant's pay?

'*Gu Nana* has no money in hand,' Bingfa's wife told him as if imparting fresh news.

'I've tried everywhere,' he said.

'Wong won't?' his wife mumbled gazing at him.

He gave his head a shake and batted his eyes once. 'Went to Fung Yungta yesterday.'

'Who?' said his wife.

'Got his name from Little Soochow.'

She knew her brother's difficulties, the shop was already mortgaged. What she could not understand was they had always made much of the Yaos being known everywhere, then how was it that a Yao's wife's family did not have enough credit to borrow on? Her brother may be a simple man, he was after all a native of Shanghai and had managed all these years. It must be that this time husband and wife had decided to make her pay, since she had to have it.

'Perhaps if *Gu Nana* talks it over with *Gu Ya*,' his wife said.

58

'Him!' she spat out the word.

'It's difficult too, *Gu Ya* lives downstairs just now,' Bingfa's wife said to him. 'Best if *Gu Nana* speaks to him in person.'

Yindi said nothing. Second Master did not like any mention of money. He was defensive about it, never having handled any. If pressed he would resort to officialese, that it does not matter what they give, it is the thought that counts.

'Maybe *Gu Ya* can draw from the book-keeper's office.' She had heard about Third Master haunting the place.

'It won't do, he's never done that before. Everybody will know what it's for.'

'Well . . . keep it from the top, not the bottom.'

'You can't keep it from top or bottom. And just when everybody is waiting to pick on me.'

'*Gu Nana* has pride,' Bingfa's wife explained to him.

'Maybe Old Mistress won't mind if it's not the complete set,' he said. 'It's not as if she doesn't know how things are with us.'

'Old Mistress won't say anything but the others will laugh till their teeth fall off.' In fact she herself had toyed with the idea of going to Old Mistress—an awkward thing to do. She would never be taken seriously again. Although well-disposed towards her just now, Old Mistress was fickle with her favours just so that nobody would be too sure of himself. Besides she was bound to take the official line. 'Tell your brother it doesn't matter. No sense in slapping your own face to make it swell and look fat.' And she would give a little money, not being familiar with current prices. When the present turned out to be cheap and incomplete she would put it to their lack of taste and not knowing how to do things properly. Same with the trousseau the Yaos had bought for her, only she did not know who got the blame then.

'Best to ask *Gu Ya*. After all it's all for *Gu Nana's* face.'

'It's not just my business.' She did not have to remind them of their stakes in it. They wouldn't be the first people to get into debt to keep up with relatives. The connection may well mean a future for all their sons, official posts even. She did not want to make promises where she wouldn't have much say. But she was furious with them for not having the pluck to see it through. Now was the time to make an effort, while she had just had a son and everybody had face. If they always wanted special consideration how would they expect to be taken as real relatives?

The wet nurse came in, having had her lunch. She took the baby to the other room for its feeding but the amahs kept going in and out. Her brother could not stay upstairs for long. 'I'd better be going,' he said.

They were leaving it to her.

'Take my pearl cap and pawn it,' she said not looking at him. 'I can't get it now, Sister-in-law will take it home tomorrow.'

His wife whispered in consternation, '*Gu Nana* will have to wear it to go out.'

'If anything comes up I can always say I'm not feeling well and stay in bed.'

They were clearly reluctant. If she had to pawn something, why must it be a thing she had to have back before long?

'There's not a thing here that will not be missed. Old Mistress even asks why you haven't been wearing such and such a ring. At least the pearl cap is only for big occasions. The furs won't be needed until winter but they're bulky. How to get them out?'

His wife sighed. 'It's a lot of responsibility. What to do if we can't redeem it?'

60

'What to do? I'll hang myself, I've had enough of this anyway.' She burst into tears.

'Now, now, *Gu Nana*,' his wife begged.

'You people know what kind of a life I live here? What do you care?'

'*Gu Nana*, people will hear.'

'It was all for your sake. What did we get out of it?' he said.

'You're sorry now,' she said. 'Better to have sold her outright.'

He stood up. 'I'm going.'

'Go, and never come again. I'd rather you don't.' Every time she saw him it brought everything up all over again even when nothing was said. After all he was her brother, the only family she had.

'So I shame you by coming. Even emperors have relatives in straw sandals.'

His wife said, 'You two seldom get to see each other, can't you even keep peace when you do?'

'Whoever comes again is no man,' he said on his way out.

'Ai-ya, if you're going, go quick,' his wife said. 'All you do is make *Gu Nana* angry.'

That night when room doors were finally shut and latched Yindi took her jewellery case out, wrapped up her pearl cap and put it in the lower deck of the basket her brother had brought. His wife took it home the next morning. She came back in the afternoon and the present arrived two days later. It was taken upstairs to the anteroom. Old Mistress was not up yet. Big Mistress and Third Mistress were the first to see it. The green of the jade pieces was not deep enough. They weighed the gold padlocks and chains in their hands and examined the embroidered goods.

'Soochow embroidery, no less.'

'Hunan embroidery is better, more shadings, the flowers more alive.'

'This costs enough.'

'It doesn't hurt them to give the lamb back some of its own wool. Bringing food and all, who knows what's taken back in the basket?'

'Yes, I've noticed too, all this coming and going. One day we'll wake up in an empty house.'

The wet nurse had come as usual to milk herself in the anteroom so it would be still warm when Old Mistress got it. Waiting in the hallway she heard everything and later repeated it to Yindi and Bingfa's wife and made them very angry.

The day before the Full Month feast Third Mistress called in a woman to restring her pearl flower.

'She can work right here,' she told her amah, Old Li. 'It won't wake up Third Master. If you don't talk. But stay around, you know what I mean?'

'I know. With all sorts of people going in and out these days, it's best to be careful.'

'She knows the pattern I want. Same as the one I saw on Young Mistress Hsu.'

The rough-work amah came in to empty the spittoon and sweep the floor as she did every morning after her lady had gone to Old Mistress. Old Li spread a little purple rug over the table where the jeweller was to work. She wrapped the pearl flower with its cotton-wool pads in a big silk handkerchief and placed it on the rug. She folded up clothes and tidied up after the mistress. The rough-work amah bent down to straighten Third Master's heel-less slippers which her broom had disturbed and got a scare when he parted the bed curtains yawning, feet groping for the slippers.

'Third Master is not going to sleep some more?' Old Li asked in surprise.

'How can I with this racket going on?'

'I'll go and fetch hot water.' The rough-work amah quickly made off with the basin to be out of the way of his wrath.

He stood before the wardrobe mirror retying the wide grey-green belt of stiff webbing that tied under his shirt and hung down, the fringes almost brushing the knees. 'Hurry up, get breakfast,' he said.

'What will Third Master have?' Old Li said.

'Go and see what there is. Hurry, I'm going out.'

Old Li called out for Juyi but the slave girl must have been having breakfast downstairs too. The others were either breakfasting or waiting on Third Mistress. She herself had to go down as fast as her age, bulk and bound feet would permit. He never seemed to remember that she was no ordinary amah but someone from his wife's family, practically his mother-in-law's representative. She was constantly vexed at her young lady's inability to stand up to him. She got his own bowl, filled it with rice gruel from the common pot and waited for the cook to arrange some cold dishes on a tray. She heard people shouting for Ahfu.

'How would Ahfu be here at this hour?' said somebody in the kitchen. Third Master's ricksha-puller only came on duty in the afternoon.

'How is Third Master so early today?' the rough-work amah waiting for hot water said to her at the stove. She just grunted. She did not want the servants of the other branches to hear about him rushing out at all hours, mad about some singsong girl.

'He's down,' now they were saying. 'Call a ricksha for Third Master.'

'Going out without breakfast, without even washing?'

63

she could not help saying to the rough-work amah. It suddenly occurred to her that if he was gone there would be nobody in the room.

She puffed upstairs. The room was empty, so was the bright purple work rug on the table by the window. A thunder clap in her ears weakened her legs. She looked on the bureau and dressing-table, behind the bed curtains as if he might have gone back to bed, and in all the drawers in case she had put the pearl flower away after all. The rough-work amah brought up the hot water and helped her look, setting the kettle down on top of a spittoon.

'Strange,' she whispered, 'I came up right away, Third Master couldn't have been gone for more than a minute —how so bold?'

'Could it be Third Master took it?' said the rough-work amah.

'Hush. If these people hear you they'd say even your own people say that. They'd be bolder than ever.'

After searching all over she had to go and tell Third Mistress, first skulking at Old Mistress's door, peering around the curtain waiting for an opportunity to catch her eye. They came back together and turned the room upside-down looking. Finally Third Mistress sat down in the midst of the debris and cried.

'There's a ghost around!—in broad daylight,' Old Li said.

'I told you not to leave this room on any account.'

'Third Master wanted his breakfast in such a hurry. Old Chou had gone for hot water and there was nobody else around.'

'How is it he went out so early, today of all days?'

'Third Master is like that. Probably afraid he won't get away otherwise, with the feast coming up and all.'

Both fell silent for a moment.

64

'Miss, this has to be reported to the police. If we don't get to the bottom of this I'll never wash the mud off me, not if I jump into the Yellow River.'

'I'll have to tell Old Mistress first.'

'Ask Old Mistress to lock the front door and have the whole house searched from top to bottom. Nine out of ten it's still here.'

Their eyes met. 'They have a gall,' Third Mistress whispered between clenched teeth.

'Getting bolder and bolder.'

'It's that sister-in-law of hers.'

'Who else is there?'

'It's not the wet nurse. She's over there giving milk.'

'It's that sister-in-law.'

Third Mistress rushed back to Old Mistress's room.

'What's the matter?' Big Mistress whispered seeing the look on her face.

She did not say anything. So Big Mistress left the room on some excuse. The slave girls also slipped away one by one. She told Old Mistress when they were alone together. Old Mistress sat perched on the edge of the rosewood couch hunched up and frowning, her long pipe in one hand and a round fan in the other. She gave her head a slight shake at the talk of getting the police, batting her eyes at the same time and looking away, making it clear that it was out of the question.

Third Mistress started to weep again. 'Nothing of the sort has ever happened before. Old Li has been with my mother for thirty years and the others have been here as long. The slave girls we've watched them grow up. They'll all get a bad name if the matter is not cleared up. Old Li is in such a state she wants to hang herself.'

'It's up to you to reassure them and keep them quiet,' Old Mistress said. 'This is not a thing you can say of

65

anybody, high or low. And what if there is real proof? The matter will really get out of hand then. If word gets out nobody will have face. Things are a small matter after all. Something lost, just call it a loss and let it go at that.'

Third Mistress still stood there crying.

'Now don't feel bad, just be more careful in future. In a big family like this with so many people around you just have to be careful of your things. Go and speak to your servants before they start talking wildly.' She rapped her pipe on the rosewood knocking off the ashes.

Third Mistress had to go back to her room and tell Old Li to send the jeweller away when she turned up, just say it did not need restringing. Instead Old Li whispered the whole story to her downstairs, growing more and more excited with the telling. After the woman was gone she started to yell around in the kitchen, 'This is too much, to get a tooth knocked off and have to swallow it. What about us servants? We're all under suspicion when anything gets lost. I'm supposed to look after my young lady's things, how am I going to face my mistress?' She was speaking of Third Mistress's mother. 'But who would have thought we'd fall into a den of thieves? One can be a thief forever but one can't be on guard against thieves forever. They got used to taking things from their own rooms, no wonder they've got bolder and bolder and started on other people. My young lady happens to be good-natured. Eating persimmons you pick the softest. I'm not to talk but what do I care? So long as you'd risk being cut into little pieces you can even drag the emperor off his horse.'

When Third Mistress got to hear of it she told Old Li, 'You're making things impossible for me. Haven't I got enough to bear as it is?'

Old Li said no more after this but the news was already out. Yindi wanted to go and have it out with Third

Mistress in front of Old Mistress at once. Bingfa's wife had to hold her back bodily.

'You'd put yourself in the wrong to begin with. They'd say you lower yourself to argue with servants, and make a scene in front of Old Mistress because of some servants' gossip. You'd play right into their hands. These people are always the worst. Their mistresses wouldn't dare say such things and Old Mistress would never listen. As long as Old Mistress knows.'

Yindi did not answer. The trouble was Old Mistress must also think the same.

She wept all night. The feast next day was difficult play-acting although she was not given any special attention, just one of the busy daughters-in-law. The baby appeared briefly carried by the wet nurse. Her brother dined with the men downstairs knowing nothing and sent word up to ask his wife to get ready to leave. His wife could not wait to go but she was a bit afraid to leave Yindi alone just now. She gave the wet nurse a special tip secretly asking her to keep watch at night. A good thing Second Master was moving back tomorrow. On her way down she was asked to take home a big barrel of water-melons and another of assorted fruits fresh from the family land. For the children, Old Mistress sent word through the amah. The men servants got them two extra rickshas to carry these.

Third Master had to be home for the feast. After the party his wife was in tears again telling him about the pearl flower; she had scarcely had an opportunity before this.

'The servants are not going to let it go at that,' she said. 'They're going to hire a round lighter. Old Li is going to pay half, the others pool together for the other half.'

He looked at her from under knitted brows. 'What a

67

silly waste of money. These people. Their money doesn't come easy and they go and waste it like this.'

'It's their money. They just want to clear themselves.'

The round lighter cuts out a round piece of white paper, sprays it with a mouthful of water that he had made sacred by some ceremony and sticks it on the wall. He gets a little boy in the audience to stare at the paper. If he stares long enough he sees the image of the guilty person.

'I'm not going to have all this hocus-pocus in the house.'

'Oh, I suppose they'll do it in the kitchen after dinner. It won't interfere with anything. Old Mistress knew. She didn't say anything.'

While he had never believed these superstitions he felt uneasy. Though not much of a scholar he was familiar with the quotation from a famous Confucian with regard to the supernatural, 'Better to believe there is than to believe there is not.' It was only sensible to play safe. The next day when he was playing mahjong in a singsong house he asked Tien, one of the hangers-on, 'You know anything about this round light thing? Is there anything to it at all?'

Tien immediately cited a few cases in which people had turned to the round light as a last resort and found the thief although more often it did not help to know what he looked like when he came from outside.

'Is there any way to break the spell?'

Tien saw that he had got him frightened. He had guessed why he asked. Young men who did not have enough money to spend often stole things from home to pawn or sell. 'There is a way but I don't know if it works. Smear pig's blood on the face and the face won't appear.' Pig's blood is one of the filthy things used as antidotes for witchcraft. It seems that only filth can kill the mystery, the aura.

68

The day that the round lighter was to come, he went and got a room in a small hotel where there was no danger of running into anybody he knew. He asked for a bowl of pig's blood. Without turning a hair the bellboy answered that this was not the hour for slaughtering pigs. The blood left over from this morning would have been sold out long ago. However a big tip worked wonders. The man returned with a bowl of blood but what was it really, he thought, and whose?

He asked for a mirror, locked the door and applied the thick liquid to his face generously. It smelled foul. He lay down but could not sleep, lying on his back careful not to rub against the pillow and spoil the crimson mask. As it dried it tightened and pulled at his skin. It was the busiest time of night at the hotel. Several mahjong parties were going on. Mahjong tiles being stirred for another game sounded like surf. Every now and then a tile was slapped on the table with its name barked out. In other rooms girls were singing bawdy songs, the mincing falsettos quite drowned by the accompanying Huns' fiddle. The window opened to an alley smelling of urine. He tried to keep it closed but it was too hot, he was afraid his perspiration would ruin the make-up.

A hawker went down the hotel corridor chanting, 'Duck gizzards! Ducks' ten odds and ends!'

'Buy white orchids!' a young girl peddled flowers from room to room. She tried his door, then banged on it. 'Want white orchids, Mister?'

These flower girls were not above stealing if you let them in and fooled around with them.

The noises subsided somewhat in the small hours. Some of the unwanted women still loitered in the hallway chatting and flirting with the bellboys putting off the beating that awaited them when they went home emptyhanded.

He had no intention of staying all night. Judging that the danger was well past he unlocked the door and called for a basin of hot water. Somebody down the hall was ordering two bowls of pork chop noodles and shuffling back to bed in slippers. After he washed the water was red. The room reeked of blood as if there had been a murder.

He brought a few bedbugs home with him. Third Mistress soon woke up scratching. She rang for Old Li to help her look in the bed. Old Li pulled the lamp cord to bring the light over and searched sleepy-eyed all over the blankets, turning back the soft Formosan mat of purple and yellow plaids.

'How did the round light go?' Third Mistress asked. 'Move over,' she told him.

'One thing about it, there's no trickery. He just picked a little boy out of the crowd, a child from across the street, eight years old, and told him to watch the paper on the wall.' Children are pure, so they have clean eyes able to see ghosts and spirits invisible to grown-ups. Virgin boys are specially pure.

'Did he see anything?'

'At first he couldn't. It took about an hour, then he said he saw a red-faced person.'

'Does it sound like anybody we know?'

'That's the funny thing. He said there were no eyes or nose, just a big red face.'

'Why, it's frightening,' Third Mistress said half laughing. 'What else did he see?'

'That's all, nothing else.'

'How do you mean red-faced? Just ruddy or really red, like the mask worn on stage?'

'Very red he said.'

'Well, the thief should be red in the face. Was it a man or woman?'

'He said he couldn't tell.'

'What's the matter with this boy? Is he near-sighted?'

Third Master suddenly said with a giggle, 'Maybe he's not so pure and his eyes are not so clean.'

'You!' she spat the word at him.

He was exhilarated by his narrow escape. A good thing he had taken precautions; he had felt such a fool going through all that.

7

The sixtieth birthday of the long-dead master of the house
was celebrated posthumously in the Temple of the Bathing
Buddha. The women drove there in a string of open
carriages with a few close relatives. The men of the house
had gone on before them. Yindi rode with the baby, the
wet nurse and an amah and slave girl. The ermine lining
showed white around the edges of her high collar cutting
across the deep pink plane of the cheek. Everybody turned
to look, startled in spite of the others that had gone before
her, young faces encased in the same pearl cap and bars
of heavy rouge. Between cap and collar only a rhombus
of face was left to be seen. The rouge was not so obtrusive
on her, being darker. It was a crimson shadow on her and
gaudy pink spots on the others making them look like
candy dolls. The calvacade and the baby marked her high
respectability and the rouge placed her as a northerner.
There was no danger of her being mistaken for one of
those singsong girls that drove to Chang Park for tea. Still
it was a theatrical look; she felt they were a troupe of
players incongruously out under the sun sailing along the
traffic. She was acting too and enjoyed it, posing as the
loved and admired one.

Plane trees lined the wide asphalt streets, the leaves
coming down in droves. As you looked down the long
straight road they sounded as if they came from very high.
She half gasped smiling at all the yellow hands fluttering
down to touch her and just missing. The rickshas and
carriages and the people dodging them, trailing long
shadows criss-cross, gave the impression of fleeing the
golden shower. A shop sign of blue cloth hanging out of a

second storey window bellied out in the wind and caught the sun on its lower corner. The afternoon sunlight on the old blue cloth looked sad, it was just passing. The day was perfect and to no purpose, like her beauty.

The monks in their ceremonial saffron robes lined up outside to welcome them with folded palms, like a frieze running along the temple wall of the same colour. Alighting from the carriages the three daughters-in-law stood out in their scarlet panelled skirts, being the only ones entitled to wear them on this occasion. Their sheath jackets were violet, turquoise and apricot respectively. They all wore the long necklace called the many-treasured chain, twisted ropes of pearls with rubies, emeralds and sapphires woven in. It ended in a large pendant of pearls and gems strung into a variation of the swastika that looked exactly like a dollar sign. Fully four inches high, dangling heavily at the navel it gave their reedy figures the appearance of a forward slouch. Old Mistress was proud that all the relatives said she had the prettiest daughters-in-law and argued endlessly which was the most beautiful. Yindi was the most striking, but some thought Big Mistress looked sweeter and Third Mistress more delicate and both had a fair complexion. She was just Second Mistress, people never seemed to remember who her husband was. He was rarely mentioned and then always in hushed tones with a grimace, 'It's the soft bone disease, but nobody really knows what's wrong with him.' The family did not encourage too many questions and he seldom appeared, just often enough to be no mystery. What she liked best about going out was to be merely one of the three.

They had reserved the temple for today. Mahjong tables were set up in the side chambers. They had more relatives than ever this year, so many were fleeing the revolution seeking shelter in the foreign settlements. She had heard

73

about revolutionaries making trouble, wild youngsters mostly. Here in Shanghai under the protection of the foreign settlements they attracted more attention than elsewhere with their own newspapers and their speechifying plays, called 'civilized plays' because they were imported, at a time when the reformers deemed most native things barbaric. Those shows with just talk and no singing were very much the vogue just now but she had yet to see one. The Yaos never went, not just because of politics. The civilized actors, as they were called, including female impersonators who still took all the women's parts, were notorious for the number of their affairs with singsong girls and concubines. It couldn't be these groups that were now forcing the emperor to abdicate? People said it was all because the premier Yuan Shih-kai was a traitor. Of course the court was a mess. The Yaos and their friends had been out of government a long time. Old Mistress seldom spoke of the present trouble but when she did there was a bitter satisfaction in her tone.

The sense of disaster was too general really to worry anybody, least of all the daughters-in-law. It did occur to Yindi that the Yaos were no longer the same as before. It had always been assumed that any Yao boy would be given a post when he came of age, in memory of the late premier. Big Master had resigned after serving as a district governor. Third Master had not been interested, like his father before him and Old Mistress would just as soon they stayed out of the dangerous game. Yindi had thought her son would be different. Now she felt a chill in the air without any perceptible change around her, gayer in fact with more relatives and parties. It was the end of hope for her brother's family too. There was just the money, what was left of it and she'd be waiting for it till her hair was white. But what was the use of thinking? As the old saying tells women, 'Married a chicken, follow the chicken; married a dog, follow the dog.'

She was out on the temple porch with Second Mistress Sun watching the children play, chasing around the courtyard with little slave girls. A boy fell down crying. His amah hurried forward to help him up and rub his palm and knees.

'Beat the ground, beat the ground,' she said slapping the stone pavement, 'it's all the ground's fault, it hurt Master Lung.'

Third Mistress could be heard whispering with Old Li at the moon gate at the end of the porch, 'Not here yet. . . . Chang Fa is back. . . . Chang Fa is no use, send somebody else. . . .'

'Looking for our Third Master again,' Yindi said.

When Third Mistress joined them at the railings Second Mistress Sun teased her, 'Missing Third Master already?'

'Who's like you? Always together, two in the same pair of pants.'

'Not us, we quarrel every day.'

'Who don't quarrel?'

'You and Third Master respect each other like host and guest.'

'Our Third Mistress is famous for being a good wife,' Yindi said. The magic of the day's outing and the company of other young women had even seemed to put the sisters-in-law back on good terms. 'Our Third Master takes advantage of her.'

'What can I do? Even Old Mistress can't control him.'

'Well, as long as it's out of your sight,' said Second Mistress Sun. 'What the eyes don't see is clean.'

'In fact I'd rather he stays out. Those few days when he's home, Old Mistress scolds if I so much as come back from lunch with my hair a little mussed,' she whispered. They all giggled. 'As if anybody could sink so low.'

'I won't guarantee, with your Third Master,' said Second Mistress Sun.

'We seldom ever.'

This was young married women's talk, difficult for Yindi to put a word in, so of course she must. 'Who'd believe you?'

'We're not a loving couple like you and Second Master,' Third Mistress returned immediately to put her in her place as an outsider on account of Second Master.

She blushed at the very idea of him and herself in bed. 'With us it's really almost never. I can swear, can you?' she said belligerently. 'Third Mistress do you dare swear?'

'Swear what? When you just got a son.' And the pair of them burst out laughing.

'To tell you the truth I don't know how it got itself born.' The minute the words were out of her mouth she was sorry to see the speculative gleam and an inward look in their eyes. They were already repeating it to others in their mind even as they laughed. The brief respite from the constant terror of attending on mothers-in-law turned their thoughts irresistibly toward sex and jokes about sex like soldiers in a war. They usually did not go this far but they seemed to be still waiting, hoping to hear more about Second Master's limitations. Then an unmarried girl came over and they changed the subject.

'Old Mistress calls,' an amah came up saying.

They hurried in. Old Mistress was playing mahjong with Third Mistress's mother.

'Where's Third Master?' she said. 'I sent for him all this time and not here yet. Your mother wants to see him.'

'Third Master is winning at mahjong. The others won't let him go,' said Third Mistress.

'Let him win a bit more,' her mother said.

Her little brother came up to the table and Old Mistress told him, 'Go join the men outside. Brother-in-law is winning, tell him to give you a bonus.'

'Brother-in-law is not there.'

'You didn't see him?'

'No, they said he hasn't come yet.'

'Then what's this about playing mahjong? What tricks are you people up to?'

Third Mistress dared not answer. Her mother was beginning to see the situation. 'What does he know, a child this big. He must have got confused, so many people out there.'

'Not here all this time. His own father's birthday. What kind of a family is this? What would Mistress-in-law think? You too, you'd even help him keep it a secret, can you blame him for getting bolder and bolder?'

Third Mistress's mother smiled slightly and said no more. She was not in a position to make peace as her own daughter was being scolded. Nor could Old Mistress slur over the incident with so many relatives watching. Some had just come from the interior and had heard about Third Master. If she passed it over lightly they would have more reason to blame it all on her over-indulgence.

Third Mistress stood rooted to the spot. Yindi and the amahs and slave girls also stood frozen, afraid to draw attention to themselves by the least sound or movement. The games went on but the players had ceased to call out the name of the tiles.

In time Big Mistress came up and reported, 'Third Master was here earlier on. He's gone to the North Station to see Old Mr Sung off.'

This was not the first time they had made use of Old Mr Sung whose wife was not in town. He had his concubine with him but concubines did not pay visits, so whatever they said about him was in no danger of being contradicted. He might be here in the temple this very minute but Old Mistress would not know. She did not look up from her game. Big Mistress stood still behind one of the chairs, drawn into the magic circle of uprights around the table.

All the games went on in silence until someone discarded a tile which had not turned up for some time. Old Mistress snapped it up crying 'Eat!' and inserted the five stripes between the waiting jaws of her four and six stripes. After that the atmosphere eased a little.

'It's so nice and quiet around here, I would have liked to take a house here, only they say it's too far out,' said Third Mistress's mother.

Everybody had something to say on the housing in Shanghai, cramped compared to the interior. Big Mistress and Third Mistress moved around tentatively on little errands. Yindi saw the wet nurse standing at the door and went up to her.

'Have you had noodles?' she whispered. 'Go get some birthday noodles.' She took the baby from her. 'Old Hsia will hold him while you are gone. Where's Old Hsia? Let's go and find Old Hsia, Little Monk.' The baby was called Little Monk. He was already enrolled as a novice in the Temple like his father and uncles when they were little, to deceive Buddha into taking special care of them.

> 'Walk, walk—
> Walk to the street,
> An orange eat,'

she chanted to the rhythm of her steps. They went out to another courtyard. The leaves had turned, rustling

78

against the old red railings. Homing crows were cawing overhead. It was still light but the moon was already out, a yellow half-burned blotch on pale blue silk. The main palace of the Buddha was here up a broad flight of stone steps, all the carved panelled doors silently open. She was so full of herself and this lovely day it ached gently like milk-laden breasts. She held the baby tighter wishing it was a cat or Pekinese dog or just a pillow so she could squeeze it hard.

Aproned men carrying flat poles trooped in and filed past her on the porch with eyes downcast. Round high boxes of unpainted chip swung at each end of the poles. The name of the restaurant was written in large black characters on the boxes. They were sending down the non-vegetarian dinner which could not be cooked in the temple. She had to be there when dinner was served. It was getting late.

She wandered across the courtyard around the huge iron incense pot on its stone pedestal. Row upon row of names were engraved on it in small fine characters, donors who had this incense pot made, '*Mrs Chan*, née *Wong; Mrs Wu*, née *Chow; Mrs Hsu*, née *Li; Mrs Wu*, née *Ho; Mrs Fung*, née *Chan*. . . .' The purposely characterless names became a bit depressing seen *en masse*. These were the women who went in for good works pinning their hopes on the next incarnation. She had the feeling that if she looked more closely she would find her own name there, cast in iron. Maybe she had come across it without recognizing it.

The corridor walk with scarlet pillars and swastika railings ran straight on into another courtyard through the moon gate. When she saw Third Master coming it suddenly seemed endless like the repetitious vista in a mirror facing another mirror. He wore a large cornelian on his

79

cap set squarely over the brows. His belted riding gown of
velvet-embossed coppery silk just reached below the knees
showing the brown silk pants tied tight at the ankles. He
walked straight-backed but with a rush in the strides, arms
hanging down, the half-fists curled back into the narrow
sleeves, ready to drop a curtsy to any elder that might
happen along, bending one knee to touch the ground with
a fist. He had seen her. He seemed to come miles towards
her looking at her, smiling. She could only talk to the baby
in her embarrassment.

'Look who's coming, Little Monk. See? See Third
Uncle?'

He did not speak until he came near. 'How is it you're
here all by yourself, Second Sister-in-law? Waiting for me?'

'Pei!' she made a loud spitting noise in his direction.
'Waiting for you—everybody's waiting for you, as worried
as ants on a hot pot, and you out having a fine time.'

'Why, wasn't I supposed to be with the guests outside?'

'Until your precious brother-in-law said you weren't
there. Old Mistress was angry.'

He put out his tongue and made as if to shrink his neck.
'I won't go in then, I'd be asking for it.'

'You don't care anyway, just run off and we get the
worst of it. Little Monk, don't you copy Third Uncle
when you grow up.'

'Second Sister-in-law is always ready with a lecture.
How old can you be? You're younger than me.'

'Who says so?'

'Of course, aren't you a year younger than me?'

'Trust you to remember a thing like that,' she muttered,
pleased. The baby was whimpering thrashing about. 'Aw,
aw, aw!' she crooned and rocked him, 'don't want me,
want Third Uncle? Want Third Uncle to hold you? Let's
smell faces, Third Uncle. Smells sweet.'

He bent close to sniff at the baby's cheek. As she passed it to him his hands brushed against hers and perhaps her breast, bound and levelled by a tight sleeveless shirt worn under the underclothes. It was really impossible to tell except that she suddenly turned and went in the side chamber. He followed her in. The candles and incense were lit but there seemed to be no one around. In the semi-darkness it took a moment to dismiss the idols, some of life-size, while the golden giant Buddha towered half-naked above.

'Going to pray, Second Sister-in-law?'

'What's the use of praying, with such a fate as mine? All I ask is for Buddha to take me back.' She went round the candle rack and looked down at the baby in her arms. 'Now that I have him I've done my duty to you Yaos, I'm free to die.'

He smiled at her across the scarlet-and-gilt bars and the rows of burning candles, little red ones. 'Why is Second Sister-in-law so sad all of a sudden?'

'Because we're here in front of Buddha. Since we're not meant to meet in this life let's tie a knot for the next incarnation.'

'If we're not meant to meet how did you come to my house?'

'Don't speak of it—how I suffered since I came. On top of everything there's this enemy from my last incarnation. There's no getting him off my mind and no hiding from him. It pulls at the bowels and weighs down the belly until I wish I'm dead. Today with Buddha as witness just give me a word of truth and I'd die content.'

'Why say die all the time, Second Sister-in-law? What am I to do if you die?' He was over the other side of the rack holding her from behind.

'Never a true word out of you.'

'You never believe me anyway.' He took the baby and put it down on the round blue prayer cushion. Straight-way it started to bawl. He would not let her pick it up. His hand inside the tight jacket was fretful from haste. The row of tiny paper-thin mother-of-pearl buttons on the undershirt and the innermost sleeveless shirt was set so close it was difficult to unbutton, especially groping in the dark. The struggle made the kisses absent-minded. She was so disturbed she did not know what she had inside until he had it in hand moulding and shaping it. She began to feel the little bird's soft beak pushing at his palm. It crouched frightened, making itself round and was shot through with a filling ache.

'Enemy,' she whispered.

The baby's howls vibrated unbearably in the stone-paved temple, probably could be heard all over the grounds. The moment was stretched so long it nearly snapped. The crying seemed to have gone on for some time and they could do nothing about it as if under a spell. There was just the most primitive desire to hide in a cave, crawl into the dusty darkness hung with lint behind the faded apricot silk apron of the table, right next to the baby on the prayer cushion. In Peking opera the courtesan went to see her impoverished lover living in a deserted temple and they made love under the god's table. That was one reason she hesitated to reach down for the baby.

'Somebody's coming,' he predicted.

'What am I afraid of? All I have is my life, they can take it if they want.'

She knew at once she had said the wrong thing. They were pressed so close she could hear a warning gong strike inside him. Theirs was such a desperate situation that they were bound to get found out before long, hardly worth while for a man when there were so many women legitimately available. But it really did not feel good to let go at this stage. He managed a half laugh.

'Lucky it's me today, Second Sister-in-law. If it's somebody else now, heh heh! . . .'

'Don't be so conscienceless.' She burst out crying pressing her face against the back of her hand on the candle rack.

'If I had no conscience I wouldn't be afraid of hurting Second Brother.'

'Your Second Brother! I don't know what sins your family must have committed, to get a son like that. It's torture for him to live, he'd be better off dead.'

'There's no need to curse him.'

'Who's cursing him? It's just my fate. I dig out my heart to show people and they say it stinks of blood.'

'You have the wrong person, Second Sister-in-law. You may not think it from looking at me the Third Yao, I'm still not that kind of man.' Holding his arm down straight, he flipped the sleeve with a crackle of silk as if shaking off a clinging hand and walked away.

In time she heard the baby crying. She picked him up and buried her face in his cloak, stifling her sobs in the padded scarlet silk that smelled faintly of milk and sweat. He was always dressed too warmly and sour with perspiration. She picked up his hat and put it back on his head. A bewhiskered tiger's face stared out over the brow of the little red cap. The protruding eyes of woven gold thread chafed against her wet face.

She dried her tears and came out on the porch. It was dark and the evening bell had just started to toll. The slow booms filled the air annihilating all thought. Peal upon peal they followed her to the inner courtyard.

The dinner tables were already set. They had brought their own dinner ware. Big Mistress and Third Mistress were busy seeing to things. She found the wet nurse and passed the baby to her. Third Master was standing behind Old Mistress at the mahjong table talking to his mother-in-law. Perhaps he would tell his wife tonight. He wouldn't dare risk it getting out? He wouldn't be able to keep it to himself for long, it wouldn't be often that he had done a handsome thing, and what a joke.

Dinner had to wait while different sets of mahjong players strove to finish their eighth round. Then there were the inevitable disputes about seating. The three young hostesses had to make quick judgements while they hustled and cajoled the guests to the exalted end of the round tables. A twenty-year-old aunt took precedence over a sixty-year-old niece and distant relatives over closer ones. People who rated better seats might grab modest ones and refuse to be dislodged, parrying with both hands, and still feel insulted if allowed to remain. Yindi was just beginning to find her way through the maze of relationships. It was especially difficult tonight, every exchange of smile and words pained her. They did not know about her yet. The matter was now in the hands of Third Mistress and her people. She had passed them the knife handle.

It was dark and draughty in the long chamber with the stone floor and just a cotton print curtain over the doorways and a weak light bulb set high up on a rafter. The scarlet tablecloths loomed big and round. She was standing up all the time reaching her chopsticks clear across to deposit food in somebody's little five-petalled silver plate.

'You eat,' the others said. 'Sit down, Second Mistress. Sit.' They pressed her down but she was up again soon. She shifted around several tables. The scattered talk and thin laughter never quite warmed up.

After the last course came the hot towels. A large oval silver box was passed around the table, the mirror-backed lid pushed up showing the face powder in the form of a hard white egg. By the time it reached her the mirror was steamed over and powder-smudged. The netted bright pink powder puff, a bit damp from use, felt cold and stiff against the face and gave her the creeps.

Mahjong was played until after midnight. In the carriage the wet nurse told her that the baby could not hold down the milk it drank. It must have caught cold. Second Master was upset about it when they got home. He had been home by himself all day.

The wet nurse said, 'He was fine all along, then I just went off for a little while, Second Mistress told me to go and have some noodles; that must be when it caught cold.'

'Who had him when you were gone?'

'Huh! who indeed?' Yindi said. 'Nobody was around, I had to hold him and go looking for Old Hsia, had no idea where she lay dying. And the little devil Laishi had gone mad chasing around with the children.'

Old Hsia claimed that she on her part had been looking for Second Mistress ever since she finished helping to prepare fruits for the mahjong players. Both amah and slave girl got a scolding from Second Master. His flat hen's squawk finally grated on her preoccupation.

'All right, all right, which baby doesn't catch cold now and then?' she said. 'The way you go around beating chickens, scolding dogs. Don't make much of him if you want him to live.' She wanted to pick a quarrel so she would not have to speak to him again tonight.

'You still have to curse him? You could have been more careful to begin with, a baby this big and he's not strong. Shouldn't have taken him in the first place.'

'Was it me who said to take him? Old Mistress wanted the abbot to see him so he could kotow to teacher.'

85

'Wet nurse, leave the door open tonight, I'll see if he coughs.'

'Yes, sir, I'll listen for it too.'

Their voices sounded far off, annoying as a trickle of ants as they made themselves felt now and then through the clothes. Her foreknowledge separated her from them as the dead were from the living. But she could not bear their busily getting ready for bed, so sure of tomorrow. Not knowing what is going to happen to one's self is not a human state. The moment became timeless, intolerable, holding her like huge pincers. What would they do to her? Concubines who misbehaved were locked up and sent to the north, not the ancestral village but the anonymity of Peking where living was cheap in one of the family's houses well-guarded by old servants put out to pasture as caretakers. What happened to wives who took a mis-step? Apparently wives never did. As much as people talked, this was never said of anybody.

With her nothing had actually happened, true. But who would believe it? And to believe it of Third Master of all people. It all came back for the thousandth time, what she said, what he said and what a fool she was. There was a small fire under her heart cooking it. She swallowed live coal down the parched throat. Towards dawn she got up and took a sip from the teapot on the table. The cold tea was bitter from standing too long. There was a big moon in the window about to go down, just behind the black shape of the two-storeyed house opposite, so big it was like a confrontation, the round face of uneven reddish yellow waiting for her here, a doomsday's sun. In the dark the room seemed much smaller. Second Master's asthmatic breathing and the snoring next door all sounded alarmingly close. The wet nurse slept with the baby in the same room with Old Cheng. With the door open tonight it

86

seemed like just an alcove. She could not help anticipating the rise and fall of the snores, a nerve-racking business, with the one slightly behind the other, now hoarse, now rich and bubbly, trailing off with an occasional groan or whistle. It sounded as if everybody was having difficulty getting through the night and had come to the narrowest part, the bottleneck.

What was that crackle and rustle? She stood listening. Old Cheng was turning on her pillow filled with green bean husks. It's good for red eyes to sleep on these beans that make a cooling drink.

She put some clothes on and steered her way carefully through the people lying parallel in the dark, each reduced to a single breath renewed with effort, wheezily, a tangled bunch of ramie stretched taut on some kind of frame, flimsier even than the helplessly offered throat. Her own was an aching iron-ringed pipe that had to be carried erect. She turned the doorknob of the store-room at the back and shut the door behind her before switching on the light. The large room closed around her at once, cosy in the warm yellow light, the unused furniture and piles of trunks arranged neatly against the walls.

Second Master would not see the light in the transom, nor could the others with a whole room in between. She set a stool on his old bed. The trouble with the bed boards was that the crash would be louder than on the floor when she kicked the stool over. There was the transom but it wouldn't do to have the door open. The other door which led to the hallway was locked. She looked around for some blanket or piece of sacking to spread on the bed but everything was packed away. Better be quick than to think of everything, the baby may start crying any minute and wake them up. It wouldn't take a moment anyway, a neighbour woman had done it when she was a child. She

87

had brought an extra trousers sash of strong white silk. It was a comfort to be able to make a household chore of it.

It smelled dusty up there, a room within a room just like the other bed. If she had done it in the summer on account of the theft it would be a protest, to clear herself. But knowing these people she wouldn't expect them to think any better of her for it. They would only say it was a common thing to do, like any low-class woman bested in a quarrel. Now she just did not care what they thought. If she still did, at least she had the satisfaction of knowing it looked as if she had something dark and horrible in her life—him if they liked, anyway some man other than Second Master. But she really did not want to think of what she left behind. A person dies as a lamp goes out. What the eyes do not see is clean. What if the world was still here in the morning, carrying on like the concubine out of the wife's sight. Everything had become tiresome, even distasteful, now that there was no more for her and she alone had to go.

8

The green bamboo blind kept moving in the summer breeze coming in the window. Sunlight tiger-striped the room and swayed back and forth. A large black-framed photograph of Second Master knocked on the wall. That time it had been he who called out and she was let down in time. She had never worn mourning white for him because Old Mistress was still alive. Heavy mourning would have been a bad omen pointing to the head of the house. Now she wore mourning for Old Mistress. She stood in front of the dressing-table with a finger in the back of her collar. The rough white cotton pricked the neck.

That had been sixteen years ago. There's the old saying, a good death is not as good as a bad life. Everybody was whispering at the time, 'Don't know why Second Mistress hanged herself.' According to Second Master they'd had words that night because the baby caught cold and he blamed her for being careless. Some said it still had to do with the theft a couple of months back. There were actually servants who heard it come up during the quarrel.

Was the third branch too scared to talk? If Third Master did let out some hints and he was the one that was always saying, 'Second Mistress Sun is unreliable', 'Eighth Mistress Liu is unreliable'—all the livelier women relatives —people would be more inclined to believe it of her because of her background. Her attempt at suicide was all the proof they would need. Was it because it was such a monstrous crime that nobody was ever accused of it? All this was her later conjecture. At the time she did not know her fate for months. Even a year later she was still not sure the family wasn't waiting for some excuse to act. Old Mistress was supposed to be angry with her just for hanging herself. What a scandal if she had succeeded. The matter was never mentioned when she waited on Old Mistress again after a few days' rest, but ever since then Old Mistress never wanted her around much. It seemed that Second Master needed more nursing now.

That year the whole family went on a pilgrimage to Pootaw Mountains to pray for his health, and chartered a steamship to the island; even he went. Only she was left behind to look after the house. But there was a movement of troops, calling back the caretakers of their houses in Nanking and Wuhu to replace the staff that had gone on the trip and patrol the house and grounds all night. As if people needed to be reminded of the loss of the pearl flower.

She had given up and got the opium habit from Second Master. It gave them some companionship and helped to kill time. His smoking had been more or less legitimized as his asthma got worse. It was more difficult for her after his death without him as shield. Women smokers were rare outside singsong houses. And it was not as if she was an old lady with failing health who had to resort to this panacea.

With men it was different. It always was with men. And they did not even have the excuse of it being the sole pastime allowed them. They should have better things to do than languish in bed with a little oil lamp and a pipe. But everybody smoked. At the singsong houses the pipe of opium was sometimes offered before the cup of tea. In Big Master and Third Master's case it first came into the open after their mother's death when they brought their opium trays into the curtained-off area in the parlour. They curled up smoking behind the white mourning curtain when they were not crouched weeping, kotowing back to mourners paying their last respects to the dead.

There was a continuation of the funeral every seven days. Troops of monks and Taoist priests took turns chanting, circling before the closed coffin. The 'seven sevens' would be completed at the end of forty-nine days. Tailors had been called in, sitting in rows making mourning clothes and the give-away sashes, working day and night. The whole house smelled of new cloth with its faint stench. A superstructure of blue and white paper flowers was built over the front gate, lighted by gas and stringed bulbs at night. The blue had run over the white after rain. The flute band played at the entrance of every mourner. The wiggly nasal squeals at a dozen different pitches blended into a single exultant blare. No wonder the same music was used in both 'red and white weddings'—'white wedding' being euphemism for funeral. This day was bound to come but it could have been too late for her. She used to squirm inside every time she saw Fifth Mistress Fung, close to sixty and a grandmother but still a daughter-in-law, standing at attention all day on wobbly bound feet in her mother-in-law's room, fetching and carrying, relaying orders, taking rebuffs with smiles and blushes. Except that she herself was not even considered good enough to serve there or anywhere in the public eye. She would have a daughter-in-law in a couple of years, a rich girl of course. How was she to put people in their place when she was so humiliated? The young couple would no longer be fledglings by the time Old Mistress died and the family was divided. The daughter-in-law would take charge and the past and future overlap leaving her no room in between.

Money would not really change anything for her except that she had been kept waiting so long and so miserably, just being on her own had come to mean everything. She had very little idea of what there was. This was not a matter a future heir could ask about. There were only chance remarks to piece together. On alternate days Big Mistress and Third Mistress went over the house accounts with cook and steward—one of the duties she was excused from—which still told them nothing of family finances. But they may pick up some information from their husbands. Old Mistress sometimes consulted Big Master on business matters. Even Third Master could not help learning something from his sessions at the book-keeper's office.

The minute Old Mistress died all her things were locked up, the keys given to the leading member of the *gung chin*, impartial relatives, those that were no closer to one of the heirs than to the other. After a decent interval they would divide and move out. Meanwhile Third Master still had access to the open account. Naturally the others were anxious to move. The house was haunted. Everybody had heard Old Mistress clearing her throat at night in her characteristic manner, khum *khum*! and knocking her pipe on the rosewood couch. Her rooms were locked up and yet the sounds came out of there. Big Master taking turns with his brother, keeping night watch over the coffin, had heard the thump of a pair of small wooden heels striking the floor upstairs, the way she got down from a chair. Yindi thought it might be that Big Mistress had keys made and got into the room. In fact she herself was also suspect.

Everybody was frightened. Still it was left to Old Mistress's brother to suggest, 'It's not healthy to live in this house. With two deaths in three years the vapour of the shades is too heavy here. You shouldn't wait till the end of the seven sevens. Call the family council now.'

All the guests had arrived but she still had to wait to be asked downstairs. Of the family itself only the men who headed each branch were to be present. She would be the only woman there. Poke her head out of the bag at last. She had never got used to her face without the bangs. An unwritten law had it that no bangs were to be worn after thirty. Gone old, she said to herself. The rough white blouse and skirt had a peasant smartness. Earrings were not worn in heavy mourning so she had stuck the stalk of a tea leaf in the hole in the ear lobe to keep it from filling up. A touch of rouge on the eyelids made them seem red from weeping and made the eyes brighter too. She hadn't gone much thinner from the opium either. For the want of something to do she lifted the lid off her teacup and drank standing up, feeling cold all over as the broad stream flowed straight down inside with a puzzling slowness. Her heart thumped in the hot tea.

'Big Master asks Second Mistress to come downstairs,' an amah came in saying.

Three rosewood tables set end to end made a long table in the parlour with everybody seated around it. The elders only nodded and made as if to rise as she came in, addressing everybody by name. Only Third Master and the book-keeper got up and greeted her back. They had left her a seat at the bottom of the table between Big Master and Old Mr Chu, his account books piled high before him, a rosy pink label pasted on each blue cloth cover. In a roomful of turquoise summer gowns and gold-flecked fans the three heirs in ill-fitting white looked slightly ridiculous together, overgrown orphans, especially Third Master who seemed to need a haircut, the way bereaved sons were supposed to. Men did not wear pigtails any more but he kept his hair long enough to tuck behind the ears like the girls who had cut their hair. Now that his natural hairline had grown back it set off the eyes and the black eyebrows. She had scarcely looked at him for years. He had gone thin so that his mouth protruded. It made him look more manly. A search party had been sent out for him in all the singsong houses when Old Mistress died.

Ninth Old Master at the head of the table made a little speech on the advisability of having this settled before the burial. He stood ninth in the clan but he was the only brother of the old master of the house. Like the other *yi lao* here, the surviving mandarins, he had kept his pigtail coiled and tucked out of sight under the black satin cap as a compromise. He was small and slight with a pale baby face, quite beardless and did not.look his age. He leaned sideways in the rosewood armchair, half reluctant and withdrawn; she had seen him just like this at New Years and festivals when he had to sit there to be kotowed to.

Old Mr Chu started to rattle off a list of acres, shares, bank accounts, trunkfuls of silverware. Every time he paused to address the head of the table he half rose and took off his tortoise-shell glasses, a sign of age and a presumption to wear in front of one's elders and betters. Now he had come to Third Master's withdrawals from the open account, apart from the two times Old Mistress had personally settled his debts. Yindi was never even sure that these counted as loans. Evidently it came as no surprise to him. He took a sip of tea and removed a tea leaf from his lower lip. It was gratifying to see him face to face on his day of reckoning. He had raced it all these years as if he couldn't spend money fast enough. Now it was here in front of him. So was she. The reflected glare of their cheap white cotton clothes threw a wan light on the face. She knew he was aware of the little smile that she held down. Surely they were not going to leave him nothing. Did Old Mistress know? Hard to tell. More and more toward the end there had been many things she preferred

94

not to know. Perhaps nobody quite knew what was going to happen when the time came. It stood to reason not to let it all go to pay his other debts. Still it must have taken some doing on Big Master's part. Elders did not like to take it on themselves to disinherit a son. Besides Big Master was deep in debt himself, only he cared more about face.

They worked it out that Third Master still had over four thousand dollars left and would get it in land.

'Land is the one sure base for a new start, and the best retreat,' said Ninth Old Master.

He got the choice land around Wuhu. Hers was up north. He got his full share of his mother's jewellery for keepsakes. This was stretched to cover the gold bars and gold leaves.

'Stocks and bonds take manœuvring. The second branch has no man. For their convenience they'll have less of these and make it up with land and housing properties.'

Finally came a lull in the readings which turned out to be the end. She had had time to get the drift of it and make up her mind although she had to stiffen her scalp to make herself speak.

'Ninth Old Master, this is too hard on us.' In the sudden silence, her woman's voice sounded unnaturally thin, flat as a razor-blade. 'In times like these, a war every year, it's difficult to get money from the land up north. Houses also have to be in Shanghai to be worth anything. As Ninth Old Master said the second branch has no man. A woman is a crab without legs and the child is still little. There're long years ahead. What's to become of us?'

The shocked silence ground on audibly like a gramophone after the record had finished. All eyes flitted away from her to stare into space.

95

Ninth Old Master cleared his throat. 'It's true what Second Mistress said about the times being bad. The fact that times have changed has to be taken into account. Naturally you cannot keep up the old way of living as when Old Mistress was alive. Nowadays who doesn't think of retrenching? A good thing you have a small family. I didn't make the decisions for today. All of us helped to make these arrangements, and I may say at considerable trouble. Bills should be settled openly between brothers. On the other hand moderation is in our family tradition. After all it's all among your own flesh and blood. One pen cannot write two Yaos. What do you think, Tzu-mei? Now, you're their maternal uncle. What you say ought to carry more weight.'

Old Mistress's brother bowed slightly and repeatedly in his seat smiling. 'As long as Ninth Old Master is here, we'll have to trouble Ninth Old Master. After all, I'm an outsider.'

'You're the closest kin, their mother's brother from the same womb.'

'She was a Yao. I'd be speaking out of turn in front of so many Yao elders.'

'What do you say, Ching-huai?' he turned to another Yao. 'Don't let me shoulder all the blame. It's a grave charge, bullying widows and orphans.'

She reddened with tears in her eyes. 'I was so upset I may have offended my elders. It's not that I can't stand hardships—what are we to do when there's just not enough to live on? Poor Second Master has only this bit of blood and bones left in the world, the child has to have tutors, then there's his engagement and wedding, all the big things coming up. If I don't do right by him how am I to face Second Master when I die?'

He shouted her down, 'What am I to do, Second

96

Mistress, if you insist it's not enough? And what if there's really not enough? If you're to take more who's to take less?'

She started to cry. 'All I ask is one fair word from Ninth Old Master. Who can we turn to with Old Mistress gone? As long as Old Mistress was here even if the sky falls down there's the tall one to hold it up with his head. Now what are we going to do, a woman with a child in tow living on some dead money, with just outgoings and none coming in.'

He jumped up. 'I wash my hands of the whole business.' He kicked the marble-inlaid armchair over with a crash and walked out.

The men looked at one another up and down the table except for the two brothers slumped in their seats avoiding everybody's eyes. Then they all got up and hurried after him.

She sat there crying. 'My husband, dear person, how cruel you are!' she wailed. 'Leave us all alone in the world. Poor you, never had a single happy day when you were alive. Whatever you did wrong in other lives you paid for it. Haven't you suffered enough, your son has to be trampled down too? What sins were they that you never finish paying for, dear person?'

Old Mr Chu was the only one who stayed. He could not leave his valuable account books and it would be rude for him to just walk away. 'Second Mistress. Second Mistress,' he pleaded.

'I want to go and explain to Old Mistress, her spirit can't be so far away yet. I'll catch up with her. Where's Little Monk? I'll take him with me to kotow to Old Mistress. His father's only seed and I had to stand there and see him get trodden down. I'll tell Old Mistress I'm sorry I failed the Yao ancestors, I'll ram my head against the coffin and follow Old Mistress.'

'Second Mistress,' he begged. It would be impudence if he were to call for a woman to wait on her or for a cup of tea, making light of her grief, or to say anything at all besides 'Second Mistress' in an urgent whisper. Beads of sweat stood on his forehead. He hovered round her in circles, took off his black satin cap to fan himself and fanned her instead.

9

'Put off until after the burial, and still divided exactly as before,' she told her brother and his wife the first time they came after she had moved, in stage whispers hissed across the room. Anybody who has lived in a big family could never get over the habit of whispering. 'Ninth Old Master wouldn't come. Somebody even said I should hand him a cup of tea and ask his pardon. I asked who had said this, and only then heard no more of it. I don't care, I tell everybody I see—why, we did get less. Just look at where the others moved to, a foreign house and garden for each wife and concubine.'

'*Gu Nana's* house here is good,' Bingfa's wife said.

'This house is cheap,' she said.

Hers was an old foreign-styled house like everybody else's except this was in an alley, a dingy cement row. There was no bathroom but the white woodwork and sliding double doors downstairs had been fashionable once. Now that she had a house of her own at last she didn't do much about furnishing it, not just to prove that she did get less, but also because she did not like to show her own tastes for fear of being laughed at as the new rich. These people, as she said, the one thing they can do is laugh at others. Even the inherited things were not on view unless they had been in use all along, lest it be said that she was so pleased with the crumbs that fell to her. Her original rosewood suite was now downstairs in the parlour, leaving her own room quite bare. The big ornate bed was getting to be an old curiosity; she had it put away. Without going so far as to buy a brass bed like everybody else she used an old iron four-poster. Some plain tables and

99

chairs were set by the window on the other side of the large room. Everybody sat so far away, looking at one another under the forty watt light they all seemed to have a strange darkness in the face. There was a mixed feeling as in a reunion after a war amidst ruins. She sat on the opium couch, the only new piece of furniture because there had been no such thing in the house before, with the ban on opium. Simple as it was it stuck out guiltily like an unmade bed, which was what it looked like, with just a thin white pad on it and two pillows on the inner side along the wall. It added to the makeshift refugee feeling.

'It's nice here, and lots of room,' Bingfa's wife said. 'When *Gu Nana* has a daughter-in-law and many grand-sons she'll need all this space too.'

'That would be some time yet.'

'It won't be long now. Seventeen this year isn't he? Two years older than our Ahmei.'

The reference to their daughter was not lost on her. 'He's still too young. Nowadays they don't marry early. The boys in the eldest branch are well over twenty and not yet engaged.' Mentioning his Yao cousins immediately put a deep gulf between them.

'It doesn't matter with boys,' Bingfa's wife murmured. 'When the time comes *Gu Nana* must be careful to find out everything—best if the families know each other. She'd also be a companion to *Gu Nana*. It must be lonely here sometimes.'

'Of course, haven't I learned enough of a lesson from matchmakers? As to being lonely, after so many years in their family you know there're worse things than loneliness.'

Ahmei came in holding her little sister by the hand. They had only brought the younger ones today. Her son was next door teaching the little boy to play draughts.

'Don't you want to watch them play?' Bingfa's wife asked the girls.

'Don't understand,' Ahmei said.

'Stupid,' her mother said smiling. 'Her little sister is the bright one.'

'Come here,' Yindi called to the little girl and felt the back of her neck. 'Ai-yo, how is it so sticky?'

'She had her bath before she came,' her mother said smiling defensively, a bit embarrassed. 'Sweated all over again running around.'

She was ticklish and twisted away, the stiff little pigtails all over her head brushing against Yindi in turn. She suddenly hugged the child convulsively and kissed her.

'She's the only one among the lot that looks like Aunt, no wonder Aunt loves her,' said her mother. 'How about giving you to Aunt for a daughter? Aunt has no daughter. We'll leave you behind when we go, all right? Eh? All right?'

The child did not answer.

'Have some sweets,' Yindi said. 'Pass us the cured plums, Elder Sister.' Ahmei brought the glass dish over. 'Take these next door,' she gave the child an extra handful and lay down to fill her pipe with an opium pellet.

All eyes in the room were naturally focused on her feet as she lay crosswise with her head to the wall. Trousers were getting shorter and much wider. She dressed conservatively but even she showed her ankles, whittled slim, in white cotton stockings. No silks were worn in mourning as silkworms meant the taking of lives. The grey cloth shoes were padded at the tips to look like the fashionable 'half-large' feet, the bound feet let out. She did not make it as long and lumpy as some did and the feet, once said to have come out well from the binding—as they often didn't—remained shapely. Bingfa felt a little uncomfortable, the more so because it was his own sister. He was an old-fashioned businessman and they were the most old-fashioned of all. His wife whispered half laughing to his daughter making conversation, then they too lapsed into silence.

'What time is it?' he said. 'We better go early. Difficult to get rickshas later.'

'Yes, once they hear it's the Old City they won't go because they can't get return fares.'

'It's lonely in the Old City now,' he said. 'The dumpling shop across the way has closed down too. New Year is the only time there's any business.'

'What dumpling shop?' Yindi said.

'Right across from us, where the pharmacy was.'

'The pharmacy is gone?'

'Oh, long ago. *Gu Nana* hasn't been back for some time now. Somehow shops across the street never seem to last.' Evidently they had often drawn comfort from the observation.

'If anybody wants mine I'd sell it too,' he said.

'You should have long ago, for *Gu Nana's* sake.'

She averted her head with a little snort. 'In times like these nobody cares any more. As long as you can get by it's considered good.'

'Nowadays it's the wholesaler that makes money,' he said crossing his legs looking into space. He had friends willing to take him on, only he needed capital. He had mentioned this earlier today, the only time he opened up.

'If the pharmacy's gone then what about Young Mr Liu?' she asked.

'Just what I was asking Ahdoo's mother the other day, I said where's Young Mr Liu working now and is his mother still alive?' Bingfa's wife said. 'Funny we still call him Young Mr Liu—not so young any more.'

'Born in the year of the snake,' Yindi said.

Bingfa was startled. Of course she knew his age because of the proposed match, but she lay there smiling, her eyes half shut in the light of the little opium lamp, looking levelly at them from far away.

'Everybody's gone,' she said. 'Is the carpenter still there?'

'What carpenter?' he asked his wife in a low voice.

'Who else? That fool who came and made a row that night,' Yindi said and he and his wife both smiled embarrassedly. They remembered how the man had held on to her hand and she burned him with the lamp to make him let go.

'Who? Who?' Ahmei whispered to her mother who ignored her.

'He was drunk,' he said.

'Drunk indeed—always like that, only he wouldn't have been so bold without the wine to cover his face.'

'He's always like this, no accounting for him,' said her brother's wife. 'Not long ago his wife came up from the country to look for him. She grabbed him by the shirt on his chest and fought him from shop to street and from street to shop. He had money to shoot pheasants and none to send home.' Streetwalkers were called pheasants, wild hens.

She was shocked. And she had thought she taught him a lesson that he would never forget. He had betrayed her memory. Even having a wife in the country was an outrage, though only to be expected. She could not stand for him to have any life aside from the scene with her that night. 'He wasn't like this before,' she said.

'Always like this,' her sister-in-law said, too absorbed in the story. 'Over forty, getting on to fifty now, time to pack up your heart and take it home, everybody told him. In the end they persuaded the wife to go back.'

She said nothing and did not talk much after this. Bingfa's wife finally noticed it and did not know where she had given offence.

'Well, shall we go?' she asked Bingfa. Speaking to her husband her voice turned gruff showing some of her disappointment.

'It's still early, not eleven yet,' Yindi said.

'It's hard to get rickshas when it's late.'

She soon gave in. 'Come early next time.'

She saw them to the head of the stairs while her son went down with them. She called him by his formal name Yensheng now. He was a quiet boy. This evening on the pretext of teaching his little cousin draughts he hardly spoke to the others.

'Where's Young Master?' she asked after they had left and was told that Young Master had already gone to bed. She had a mind to lose her temper with him tomorrow. Unless he had overheard the hints of his marrying one of their girls? She wouldn't blame him in that case. They were really impossible today, couldn't wait to lay hands on her money and force their daughters on her. If the older one wouldn't do there was still the little one. In the Yangtze River the back waves push at the front waves, as the saying goes. The younger generation would shove her aside when she herself had scarcely arrived. And to talk about it when the children were right in the next room— at his age the very mention of a match could make the heart grow wild. He had been quite sensible so far, and knew enough to be afraid of her. All these years when she had been tucked out of sight in her room even servants would tread on her if they weren't afraid of her, not to say her son—how else would she have any control over him? He would go the way of the boys of the eldest branch, little devils all of them, only afraid of Old Mistress, capable of anything once out of her sight. Yensheng had enough sense to keep out of their way. Still, growing boys studying in the same schoolroom in a big house where the comings and goings were impossible to trace from upstairs—that had been a real worry. Now she got him a resident tutor of his own who also wrote letters for them on occasion. The old gentleman was over seventy but he wouldn't be studying many more years anyway and with the teacher living in and she a widow, it wouldn't cause talk.

Being left alone together all of a sudden took some getting used to. He seemed almost wary. That healthy fear of her was just as well. He'd be easily spoiled with all those examples before him and he an only son and her sole glory. But tonight she would have liked to chat a little just to take the taste of the visit out of her mouth. They never talked about her brother and his family. They upset her every time she saw them. She was going to have trouble sleeping again. She had an amah undo her hair and clean it with fine-toothed bamboo combs stuffed with cotton wool.

She was sitting at the back window. It was so hot, not even a breath of air at this hour. A steamy odour came up at night from the little alley below in slow puffs and waves, a mild pent-up smell richer than sweat. This was where the elbow of the new jerry-built alley came right up to within a foot of the downstairs window, one reason why this house was a bargain. Old City never had anything like this. There the little houses were old and not so crowded. What smells there were would be more of excretion than secretion.

Suddenly there was a quarrel going on. Blanketed by the thick warm blackness the voices sounded startlingly near, yet muffled. It could be some distance away on the street. All she could hear was a young woman bawling:

'I won't have it. I won't have it. Nobody's ever beaten me. I'm his what, he beats me?' It sounded like a child's half-forced tearless howls.

Several people spoke at once.

'Go home first, it's late,' advised a bossy woman with a Nanking accent, the only bystander whose voice and delivery seemed trained to carry. 'What you want to say can be said tomorrow.'

She got up to look out of the window and could see nothing in the solid darkness. Not even any light from the houses. Could it be because the alley was so narrow? The hubbub sounded no nearer. Straining to hear, she was furious with the amah for interrupting embarrassedly, 'It's not like in the old house with the big garden, Mistress. There you don't hear the street brawls.'

'Huh! the old house. Enough brawls inside.'

'I won't have it. I won't have it.' The young woman's wails seemed to have drifted away down the street.

'Go home and have it out with him,' advised the woman from Nanking, addressing herself more to the crowd than the couple who were apparently no longer with them. 'He's in the wrong too, could have said his say nicely. Instead when he opens his mouth it's to scold, when he moves his hand it's to strike.'

The howls faded away up some street vertical in the darkness that had the city up like a map on the wall.

When she was young she had often heard of such unions and separations, usually of people who had spouses elsewhere in the country. Somehow these things did not seem so bad among poor people. The hardships of life made their own rules. Some of those affairs lasted a lifetime. They did not have to end badly. But the people involved had to be poor, especially the woman. The man could walk in on her any time and take anything he wanted.

When you give your body over to be loved you have also given it over to be robbed and abused.

It was no good thinking of that teeming world she had grown up in. After the amah had gone to bed she moved over to the window on the other side away from the smell and continued to air her hair. It gave her quite a turn to see her face reflected in the window glass of the house opposite. Just the face alone with no hair showing, a blue-shadowed moon afloat on the dark pane. Far off and in this light she looked young and mysteriously beautiful. She could not resist smiling tentatively at the reflection raising her hand at it. It frightened her to see the face smile back at her beckoning slightly. She found herself going towards it at once. Or at least it was something that issued from the top of her head, almost ticklish in its lightness, sailed across and was gone. The face was still smiling palely at her from the dark room across the way. A ghost. Perhaps she had hanged herself sixteen years ago and did not know it.

She quickly went and lay down on the opium couch and lit the little lamp, comforting even on a hot day. The trouble with opium couches was that they were always arranged for two to lie *tête à tête*. Here as nowhere else she felt her husband lingering on. With the glassed-in flame shining into her eyes he could very well be curled up on the other side of the tray. Actually what was the difference whether he was still here or not?

Smoking more would keep her awake. She just rolled pills for tomorrow over the burner, more than she needed, weaving one brown cocoon after another to keep from going to bed. She got so tired she was beginning to burn them or let the raw thin paste drip hissing into the lamp. Here it was still a well-lighted public place. There she would be by herself in the dark, nothing to think about except for the day's grievances told over and over again in the same words. The comfort of bed soon turned into a mere awareness of the disposition of the arms and legs that stiffened and soured on her almost right away. Roll over and the rearranged pattern made itself evident after a minute, as tiresome as the ugly cotton print curtain that hid the chamber pot beside the bed. Flat on her back and the parallel white lines of the leg bones stretched out straight before her, thick from the strain. The brush strokes paused to gather strength at the kneecap and again at the ankle and thrust hard into empty black space. Despite the constant shifts her neck was cramped. Sometimes she could feel the dumb mouth inside her, lips pressed lightly against each other, unendurable just by making themselves felt. The old saying about women was 'At thirty like a wolf, at forty like a tiger.'

She just lay there lingering over the little lamp in her eyes and the whole city lying low and darkened at her feet. Perhaps it was going to rain. Every sound outside seemed to be separately wrapped and rolled in wet cloth to keep it fresh. That familiar noise was one of the panels being forced open on a boarded shopfront. Then followed the soft full-bodied splash of water on the pavement. Somebody had washed his feet and thrown out the water.

'Ae-ho . . . red-bean cake! Sweet lo . . . tus-seed gruel!' a hawker chanted tunefully in a tenor voice sweetened by distance. Steamed cakes of rice-flour studded with red beans, and sugared rice gruel with red dates and lotus seeds, midnight snack for late sleepers. The long-drawn little melody reached instantly inside her making a hollow and a silence in the heart.

She listened with her eyes on the window. He came nearer with each call. She waited with dread anticipating sadness. He had turned into the alley. She had never heard it so close, something to do with the damp heavy air. The threads of hoarseness running through the voice could be felt with a hand like the veins on a bamboo. A common pleasant voice, rather young, sang loudly, 'AE-HO...RED BEAN CAKE! SWEET LO...TUS-SEED GRUEL!' The voice hung naked and drawn out in the black rectangle of the window.

10

Clothes were sunned every summer, put off this year because the family was about to be divided, servants were uneasy about their futures and there was more danger of losing things. As the new house had no balcony the old costumes blocked the windows in shifts, her share of the court gowns and women's mandarin coats stiff with massive gold embroidery and huge jackets like satin-banded silk tents in unlikely colour combinations, comical even when she was young. The fur linings smelled remote in the warm breeze. Some of it had belonged to Old Mistress though hard to imagine, most of it nobody knew any more whose it was. It gave her a queer feeling to have them herded at her window like so many curious country people not quite looking in while she lay on the forbidden couch with her lamp and tray.

Nothing could be done with them except to air them once a year and fold them back reverently. The men's gowns were almost as bright and elaborately trimmed but with a narrower cut. Some of Second Master's more recent clothes in sober blues and browns might be made over to fit her and Yensheng. For the first time in her life he seemed a cosy convenience like anybody else's husband. What with all the married couples quarrelling, the frenzied whoring and gambling and deserting the wife for the concubine, people told her, 'You're still better off,' and now they really meant it.

Lying across the width of the couch she found herself looking at two plain silk gowns hung side by side, of peacock blue and a pinkish red. They cut a figure against the blue sky with the graceful droop of the long sleeves and the hips swaying forward a little, borne on a light wind. Every now and then the blue sleeve slapped at the red sleeve guardedly without lifting itself as if afraid to be seen. After a while the red sleeve slapped back and it was the blue one's turn to seem indifferent. At times they appeared to join hands. She was somehow reminded of herself and Third Master. They had just happened to be near. He was always teasing her. She was fool enough to take him seriously and he got frightened, that was all. She was able to think of him without flinching now that they no longer had anything to do with each other and he had lost his fortune. Sunlight touched the corner of the red sleeve. It was all so long ago.

She was either on the couch or at the window, not hanging over it brazenly but standing over to one side ready to draw back if noticed. Around tea time the hawker of bean-curd flower came and parked his stove and cupboard in the alley. He dished out the amber soup clouded by pale watery bean-curd which he just called *haw*, flower.

'*Haw* O! . . . *Haw* O!' Faraway in the late sun it became 'Aw O! . . . Aw O!' a hollow-sounding echo straight down the passage of time.

The amahs collected the water-melon seeds and put them out to dry on basket lids on the window sill. Small red seeds, the store-bought ones were black. The red brick house opposite was still older than this one and just as hemmed in by the new little slum alley. A bee flew across the long row of upstairs windows, its body golden in the sun. That was where she had seen her reflection that night. One of the windows kept banging, a desolate sound in the silence.

'How is it everybody's out all day?' she said to an amah.

'They're people who live in little homes,' said the amah. That was what they called lodgers. The house was sub-let to several families. At dusk the rooms remained dark. A bamboo pole came out of a window, clumsy in its length, groping uncertainly for a foothold on this side. A ghostly mauve blouse on the pole jerkily inched nearer, arms stiffly outspread and half tilted. She watched with some apprehension and craned her neck out to make sure that the sill it settled on was next door.

At night there was a game of mahjong in the golden room. Somehow the entire interior was open to view as in old paintings. The men stripped down to the waist looked as if they were painted on gilded paper. Those that looked on stood about or paced around with narrow golden backs above the white trousers.

She watched them as you watch birds and animals in a cage. Now that the world was rid of her enemies there were no people left. She had visitors only at the three main festivals. Relatives having ignored her all these years were embarrassed to see more of her suddenly and seem like snobs. She did not seek their company either not wishing to seem eager. There was only her brother's family. Bingfa's wife came by herself the next time, more convenient for borrowing money. She put her off. Each took turns at further confidences about her own difficulties. It was a relief when the amah came in.

'Mistress, Third Master is here.'

She was taken aback. 'Ask him to sit in the parlour. I'll be right down.'

'Now what did he come for?' she muttered to Bingfa's wife.

She came down prepared for trouble. She would like to see how he was going to blackmail her after so many years and no witness. A woman's reputation was important but so was his. He had to live off people's good will from now on. He couldn't risk such talk getting out. There was no telling what he had up his sleeve. There were still many things she didn't know in the outside world. It was bracing. Everybody likes things to happen after all. When it comes to a point when really nothing good can happen, then bad things will do. If a bad thing cannot happen to other people then let it happen to oneself.

'Why, Third Master, what made you think of coming today?' she said. 'How is Third Mistress?'

'She hasn't been so well. Better now.'

'You must have made her angry again. Now that there's nobody to control you I really worry for Third Mistress.'

'As a matter of fact she's having an easier time now she doesn't have to account for me to Old Mistress.'

'At last a conscientious word from you.'

Once they sat down and looked at each other smiling there was a feeling of security. Time had petrified their relationship so it stood between them, a prison wall and shelter.

'Second Sister-in-law has a nice house here.'

'The main thing is it's cheap. You saw how it was that day. A woman like me with a child in tow, how can I help getting frantic? Not like you, Third Master, you're used to a big coming and going of money.'

'With me it wouldn't help anyway.' He smoked a cigarette with a long holder.

'Money is a small matter; what made me angry is they don't treat people like people. All three of you crawled out of the same mother's belly, how is it the minute the mother died it's one man's world and none of the elders will say a word.'

'They'd never bother.'

'All bend with the wind.'

'Second Sister-in-law is more than a match for them, made Ninth Old Master jump up to the roof. So far there was just our Old Mistress with her chatter, he was a bit afraid of this Sister-in-law. Now there's just Second Sister-in-law who at least dares answer back.'

She knew this was meant to please her and was still duly pleased, murmuring, 'I was just too outspoken and what good did it do?'

'This is one more joke on him. There was that time when he started a newspaper to boost an actor. They ran down the rival female impersonator who had a war lord backing him. The newspaper got smashed up from top to bottom and the editor beaten up and the old master didn't dare go out for months.'

'Yes, I seem to have heard that Ninth Old Master likes to boost actors. One of the four great female impersonators was boosted up by him.'

'He only likes rabbits.' She never knew why northerners call professional homosexuals rabbits. Tzuming isn't his son.'

'Oh?' she said smiling. He had sounded so casual. Tzuming was Ninth Old Master's only son, already married. 'This I haven't heard,' she admitted. The women gossiped when they got together but never anything like this. Perhaps it was because she had no real friends among them. But she felt she was stepping into the men's world for the first time.

'He told a manservant to go in. Let him loose on the wife.'

'And the wife went along with it?'

'There must have been some understanding between husband and wife, otherwise the servant wouldn't have been so bold.'

'What happened to this man?'

'Later they let him go. It was said that when Tzuming was little he used to yell around the gatehouse, Young Master is my son.'

She half gasped laughing. To think that she herself nearly died for her guilty secret, nothing compared to this. Of course incest is something else again but it seemed to her that dallying with a servant was not much better. If that had been her they would say she was born cheap.

'And nobody said anything,' she said. He himself now, wouldn't he want to claim his uncle's fortune? Ninth Old Master was frugal apart from the promotion of actors and very strict with his son, so his inheritance was still intact. Having been a high official himself he had presumably added to it. With his prestige she supposed nobody dared sue him for a thing like this. It would only drag the family name through the mud and earn the hatred of all the relatives.

'Oh, this is an old story,' he said carelessly.

'Come to think of it, Ninth Old Master is a bit strange. . . .' Shadowy and chilly. She never could make him out except that one time he lost his temper at the family conference. Such fire, a small man like him kicking over the heavy chair, yet such a pimp and cuckold—imagine keeping that man around all those years after the son was born—why? Hoping for another heir for safety's sake? Certainly not to keep his wife occupied?

'It was the fashion among mandarins. There was this law against their going to singsong houses so they had boys to sing at their parties. But there were very few like him who couldn't stand women.'

'Ninth Old Mistress was said to have been a beauty too.'

'He made it up to her. What it comes to was adopting his wife's son.'

She laughed. 'That's you Yaos for you.'

'Well, you can't generalize. Like me for instance, I'm no use. They're the bold ones. Compared to them I the Third Yao did nothing except spend a little more money.

The fact is I was a fool,' he said smiling with no change of expression. But something in the pause that followed showed he was speaking of that time with her in the temple. He was sorry now to have held back for the family's sake. Of course he was feeling bitter. It would seem to him that he had been treated shabbily at the division of property.

She put an end to the silence returning to the subject, 'No wonder they all say Tzuming is stupid.' She had never noticed before that it was invariably said in a furtive tone with a reflective smile. She now understood it to mean that he was not a 'seed with the fragrance of books', a son of literate people. He didn't do well at his studies, nor did Big Master and Third Master for that matter.

'Does he himself know?' she whispered.

He shook his head slightly with a half-wink that dismissed a forbidden topic, as if Tzuming was within earshot. 'That fellow, there's a lot of jokes about him too.' Tzuming was strangely terrified of his father—not so strange in the light of what she now knew. But timid as he was he got into quite a few scrapes.

'Here I am laughing at others,' he said, 'I'm in a terrible plight myself. Can you lend me eight hundred dollars, Second Sister-in-law? I'll give it back as soon as the money comes from Wuhu.'

Although fully expecting this she was just as riled. She was talking and laughing with him out of good manners and sophistication. Did he think she still felt the same about him after the way he had treated her? He took it for granted just because there was no possibility of her meeting any other man. She said smiling with scarcely a moment's pause, 'Ai-yo, Third Master, after all my complaints, don't you know Second Sister-in-law is poor? And you with a rich brother and sister-in-law right there.'

'To tell you the truth, some I just don't care to ask.'

116

'I realize it's an honour, only it puts me in a dilemma, just when I'm short from moving house.'

'Lend a hand, Second Sister-in-law! I the Third Yao may owe money all over, this is the first time yet that I opened my mouth to my own people.'

'If only it weren't just now. I'm waiting for the money from the land myself.'

'Lend a hand, lend a hand. Second Sister-in-law has always been good to me.'

Is this blackmail? 'And got dog bites in return,' she said.

He grinned. 'That's why I'd rather come to Second Sister-in-law; if I get turned down I deserve it. I wouldn't take it from the others.'

Still he would not have come to her unless he was really desperate. Of course what he got at the dividing would not last him long and his creditors must be closing in on him. The end was near then and this time there was no front-row seat for her as at the family conference. In her backwaters it would take her a long time even to hear of it. Closing the door on him was no revenge. There's power in money only when it's used, given or withheld unexpectedly, never taken for granted. She had surprised herself with the sudden decision and knew at the back of her mind it was all excuses. 'I'll never learn to be like you Yaos,' she shook her head smiling. 'As long as I have a mouthful of rice to eat it will embarrass me not to help the family.'

'As I said, Second Sister-in-law is good.'

She glared at him. 'How much did you say?'

'Eight hundred.'

'Who'd have so much in the house?'

'Come, come, Second Sister-in-law, you have enough silver dollars holding down your trunks.'

'I'll see if I can scrape together five hundred.'

'Seven hundred, seven hundred,' he said placatingly. 'Maybe I can get by with seven.'

'You'll be lucky if I can find five.'

Half-way up the stairs she remembered Bingfa's wife was still here. It was going to be embarrassing to get the money out in front of her when she had just been refused a loan and after complaining to her all along about the Yaos, especially the third branch, ever since the trouble over the pearl flower when she the sister-in-law had suffered just as much. Besides a woman giving a man money —without sufficient reason, which still did not make it any better. There was nothing to do but harden her heart and keep walking up. At least that will show her nobody has first claim on me, she said to herself.

Bingfa's wife was sitting by the window playing 'catch the tortoise' with dominoes.

'This Third Master is really in a fix, with his black rice and white rice and three households,' she said as she turned away to find the key for the cabinet. Opium is black rice because it becomes just as much a staff of life. 'What can I do? I have to make a gesture for this once.'

She counted the banknotes with her back to her sister-in-law who was trying not to watch her openly. She counted too fast. One cannot short-change a debtor. Her ears burned as she riffled through the roll a second time, knowing this would make it sound even more.

'He'll come again,' Bingfa's wife said.

'There'll be no next time. Who can afford to keep this up?'

She was fifty dollars short. She turned to the stack of trunks at the foot of the bed, carved with gold dragons and red lacquer and sheathed in padded blue jackets fastened with frogs. She opened the top one to get the packs of silver dollars which 'pinned down' the corners of the trunk.

Gold and silver have powers. With four tall stacks standing here like pillars no witch could use the Five Demon Movers Method to steal anything. It took for ever to unfasten the row of frogs. Bingfa's wife had gone back to her dominoes.

She gave a little cry when the trunk lid slammed down on her hand. Bingfa's wife made as if to get up and help hold the lid, then went on rearranging her dominoes into the shape of a tortoise.

The coins packed in mulberry bark paper were so bulky she had to hold them in her pocket as she went downstairs, so that the weight would not tear her blouse. He stayed a little longer, then started up, mumbling half laughing, 'Going, got to be going,' one of his well-practised smooth exits. She could be just another aunt to elude. Everybody said the ladies were easy to cheat and even if not deceived they were too embarrassed to say no when he made a nuisance of himself. Somehow she felt easier at this familiar little scene. According to the Confucian clan law he was family while her brother was just a relative. She leaned heavily on this. Otherwise she would really feel bad about her brother. The wife was different. When he came to fetch his wife after supper she mentioned Third Master being here but would not say why. His wife said nothing. He would hear of it soon enough when they got home.

11

Like many people with nothing to do she was always impatient to get things over with. Early in the twelfth moon she hustled the servants through the year-end house cleaning and sent men out for the New Year shopping—fruit, nuts, candies, preserves, herbs, ham, salted pork, rice cakes and the thin transparent noodles used for soup, like preparing for a siege as indeed they would live off the larder for weeks. She even got the New Year flowers weeks ahead, waxy yellow plum blossoms, berries with bamboo leaves, narcissus and 'green for ten thousand years', an evergreen. There was no sense in waiting until prices soared at the flower market. The rooms were cold enough to keep the buds from blooming too early.

This being the first New Year on her own, precedents had to be set, whether to continue as before or suitably cut down, such as the number of dishes set out before ancestors. So far even the tutor got the same number of meat dishes and vegetables as his predecessor in the old house, only the cook was allowed less per table, so the food suffered. She had to save where it would not show. She was really afraid for the future and was settled down for a long siege.

She wrapped the tips in rose-red paper, dozens of little packets to leave at relatives' houses. She herself would only go to a few elders. Her son would do the rounds. Money gifts for children were put in red envelopes. She made him write inside the gold borders *Long life, hundred years* or *Longevity, wealth and influence* while she watched with an elbow on the table under the lamplight. That felt good, their first New Year by themselves.

The servant Wong Ji had taken out the tin candlesticks and incense pot and ancestral portraits. This year there were two new pictures, Old Mistress and Second Master, both photographs. An extra place was set for the old concubine who had been Old Master's mother. The arrangement involved protocol that Wong Ji was familiar with. He also knew all the birthdays and death anniversaries when a sacrificial table had to be laid. She had kept all the old staff. There would be talk if she changed servants the minute she moved out and just as bad if she got rid of them one by one. They would go to her relatives to ask for jobs and recommendations and gossip about her. A widow could not be too careful of her name.

'Northern servants are still the best,' she said. 'For one thing they don't have relatives here to come calling and hang around.'

How tired she was of the old faces who had witnessed scenes she wanted to forget. But it was a revenge too just to keep them. They made the dynastic succession more real.

She kept to Old Mistress's ways in everything except for her mouthful of smoke. And she had the opium couch put away during the New Year when her room would be on view. With the room emptier than ever and again time on her hands, she stood at the window looking out on a grey day. A cock crowed thinly in the distance like a door creaking. Cocks answered in other parts of town. Almost everybody had a chicken in his backyard ready for the feast but not here, northerners do not have chicken at New Year. The wind swept the alley clean. A large unkempt black dog wandered alone past the row of closed doors, sniffed at a tall basket of charcoal, stood up to look inside and kept worrying it until he had upset it. He burrowed in and came out with a piece of charcoal which he gnawed, dropped and examined. He walked away disappointed, but found nothing else in the alley from end to end. He returned to explore the basket further and came up with another piece of charcoal. This he ate with a loud crunch. He ate one chunk after another always picking them with a disgruntled fastidiousness, testing them by throwing them on the ground and nuzzling them turning them over.

'Mistress, Third Master is here,' Old Cheng came in saying.

So, she thought, his creditors must be hounding him with New Year at hand. New Year's Eve was the mountain pass which once gone through may earn you another year's respite. Creditors with lanterns were out until dawn collecting. Debtors hanged themselves that night.

'Tell Wong Ji to light a fire in the parlour,' she said.

With mixed feelings largely lost in the excitement she changed into a padded jacket and trousers of the same slate grey cotton bound with white braid, suitable for this stage of the mourning. There's the old saying, 'Want to be smart? Wear light mourning.' Under the lacquered hair pulled back flat the face without any make-up was deep yellow, a protective colouring in a way. She didn't look so old she thought.

She greeted him with the usual 'Ek' of pleased surprise. 'How did Third Master find time to come just now?'

'I don't celebrate the New Year. It's not like before when you have to.'

'Yes, there's really no point to it and it's going to be lonely this year. With New Year it's the more the merrier.'

'We certainly had enough people.'

'Just the concubines, sit them down and they'll make three tables of mahjong.'

He laughed. 'Not so many.'

'Yes there were. Maybe not at the same time, and that's not counting the ones outside.' When Old Mistress lifted the ban on concubines, judging her sons old enough to indulge, the singsong girls taken into the house had soon lost favour to new ones installed outside that the old lady knew nothing about. She never did keep up with them. Being trained to please they made superior slave girls. She especially took to one of Big Master's. It was 'Fourth Mistress Concubine', 'Fourth Mistress Concubine' all day long. Even the favoured daughters-in-law suffered at the hands of the wench, not to mention Yindi. She purposely brought them up now to show she no longer cared for him in the least. 'Why, we haven't even seen the two you have now.'

'They're not presentable.'

'You're too modest. Can your choice be wrong?'

'No, it was just the pranks of friends that got me into it.'

'Now who's to believe that?'

'It's true. Either that or it was to outdo somebody else. Actually I've always said why take it to heart when it's supposed to be play?'

She just smiled. 'Gone out much lately?'

'No, I seldom go out now. Getting old, not welcome any more.'

'Being modest again.'

The fire was coming up.

'Only now it's getting warmer. Why so thrifty, Second Sister-in-law?'

'Ai-ya, Third Master, go and ask around how much coal costs, with a war on up north and none coming.'

They talked about relatives trapped in the war in Peking. He took off his fur-lined gown, threw it on the rosewood divan and paced the room talking in a thin padded suit of dark blue silk. A wide stiff slate-coloured fringed belt hung down in front under the jacket where he was still flat in the belly. Once it got warmer the flowers started to give off their scent. They crowded the white mantelpiece and the little tea tables. The white double doors were slid shut because there was no fire in the dining-room. The downstairs suite was never used, she never even came down because the teacher lived on the ground floor. It smelled like a new house, clean and a bit dusty.

'Is Yensheng home?'

'He went to the Chungs. That's a southern custom inviting people for New Year dinners days ahead. Mrs Chung is from the south.'

'Mrs Chung with her looks,' he grunted.

She laughed, 'She can't be called ugly—lovely skin.' She was rotund and wore small round green glasses.

'Doesn't even look like a woman,' he complained as if outraged.

Spoken to a woman this would seem to include her among those that at least look like women, not much of a compliment but enough to make them feel cosy sitting across the room in the twilight. It had suddenly got dark. 'It's snowing,' she said.

They watched it come down like midges, dark specks on the pale grey sky. The neighbourhood shops had started to beat gongs and drums warming up for the New Year. The clerks and apprentices went at it as soon as they had closed for the day. The big gongs boomed hoarsely at a frenzied speed, dongdongdongdongdongdong, punctured now and then by a tinny clap of cymbals. Only in the pauses of exhaustion were the drums heard, like thumps of frantic toes racing in circles on a hollow floor. Unsynchronized from shop to shop but somewhat merged by distance, it had a vast sense of time running out. It paced the late shoppers carrying food parcels tied with straw that cut into their frozen hands. Shop and cook for the sacrificial table, do right by your ancestors, set the tone for the coming year, hasten home no matter how far away and be reunited. Hurried scenes in the withering year, was the old phrase for these last days of the year.

'Yes, it's snowing,' he said.

She was not going to give him anything this time and he knew it. Here was her chance to show that she was just being civil. Why pay for his conversation every time as if she was starved for company? It would not help him either to confess what straits he was in. It would only avenge her.

They talked about relatives. She was in no hurry to fill in the pauses, giving him time to think of leaving. But these silences in semi-darkness had a flavour of their own. Darkness came up as slow as honey, almost ticklishly creeping up bit by bit where they sat in this new thicker element, the half-frozen time of ten, twenty years ago. She could hear the nostalgia in his voice like a quiet smile they exchanged unseeing. She ought to get up and turn on the light before a passing servant saw them sitting in the dark. But she was afraid of disturbing the tenuous strands of the spell that bound him to her.

She got up.

'Don't turn on the light,' he suddenly said pettishly, almost with a childish whine. She had never heard him sound like this.

She smiled surprised and sat down again feeling very happy.

When she finally had to go to the light switch she had to add, 'Third Master is staying for dinner,' lest it seemed like a hint for him to leave. What could she do? It was getting on for dinner time.

125

'It's still early. When do you people have dinner?'

'We have it early.'

Sometimes asking people to stay for dinner was also the cue for them to leave. But he stayed. Could it be that he came out today to avoid his creditors, with nowhere to go? She never asked if he wanted to smoke either. A tray could be brought in here and he could use the divan. Opium smokers were not required to stand on ceremony where they had to lie down. Still it wouldn't be very nice. Anyway opium was never mentioned in his family.

The dining-room was freezing. He put his fur-lined gown on again. The amahs filled their tiny fluted tin cups with warm wine in a tin kettle.

'This will keep out the cold,' she said.

'Is this burning roses? Not bad.'

'It's just sorghum brandy from the corner shop. I put in the dried roses and let it stand for two, three months, for the New Year. I'll tell them to get you a bottle to take home. We still have some roses left.'

A handy man was sent to buy a bottle of wine. An amah brought it in together with the dried roses in a paper packet. She slid them in and they hung in a cluster at the bottleneck. Miraculously the withered tiny roses turned a luscious deep red. She had never noticed it before and would never have thought wine could resurrect dead flowers. She added powdered sugar sprinkling it like scraped ice over the blossoms on the surface. The white flakes drifted slowly down through the greenish twilight in the bottle. The bottom was soon covered with snow with one or two rose petals lying on it, a strange scene. The dead flowers that bloomed again shook her a little. She was instantly ashamed of herself, turning away from it like the immediate reaction to a bad omen, not so much dread as dislike. The drinks had brought a flush to her cheeks that burned in the cold room, more like her old face with the rouge, the face he knew her by. Her eyes slid around like a heavy liquid that had to be controlled with an effort.

'Rice for me,' she signalled an amah.

'Second Sister-in-law can drink more than that.'

'I'm out of practice, Old Mistress used to have wine at supper every day. You have more.'

The amah refilled his cup and he raised it at her. 'Dry cups.'

She finished hers to keep him company. Absurdly instantaneous and quite unconnected with the course of the wine down the system a secret warmth came up from under her like sitting on a strong lamp. She applied herself to her rice and only pressed food on him.

They were served tea in the parlour. The gongs and drums were louder. More shops had joined in after supper. He sat hunched forward nursing his tea looking into the pane of red light on the stove.

'This time of year you can't help looking backwards and forwards. I'm finished, and who's to blame? Not you.'

For a moment she was stunned trying to make out what he meant. 'What's the matter with Third Master?' she said half laughing. 'Didn't have much to drink either.'

'Think I'm drunk because I let out the truth? When was it that you came, the year of the revolution? The year before. Ever since you came I couldn't stand it at home. I had to go out all the time. I wasn't like that before.'

'Don't talk nonsense,' she murmured smiling slightly looking away.

'I only want you to know that I the Third Yao wasn't born like this. No matter what other people say, as long as Second Sister-in-law understands I'd die content.'

He sounded like he was speaking of suicide. 'Why talk

127

like this all of a sudden? It couldn't be that a clever man like you would think himself into a corner?'

He smiled back at her. 'Don't misunderstand now. All I want is a good word from you. Say it and I'll go.'

'What is there to say? What's the use of going into it now?'

'It wasn't easy keeping it to myself all these years, but I'd rather have you hate me. If it got known it'd be worse for you than for me.'

'How thoughtful of you. I nearly died.'

'I know. I wanted so much to tell you afterwards, if we die we'd die together.'

'That's what you say now. Who knows what you told other people?'

'If I ever said a word I'm not human.'

This she more or less believed after continual soundings these many years. There'd be a difference if anybody knew at all. 'Who can tell about you?' she muttered in a tone of dismissal.

'Funny, the one nice thing I ever did in all my life. Heaven's retribution I suppose.' He stood up and was going to get his gown. 'You're hard,' he said looking at her. 'I always liked hard women.' He reached for her hand. 'I'm going, just say you understand.'

'What is there to say? My life is over anyway.' She did not believe him but it was good to bask a while in that soft religious light that had suddenly flooded over the years giving everything a meaning and a reason for all the pain. Already she was speaking as if she did. Like a disbeliever in a temple she was bowing with folded palms just because the ancient bell was tolling and the incense was sweet.

Her hands remaining in his had said enough. But she could not meet his eyes, afraid that deceit would be faced with deceit. Her cold hands in his were real. So was the grip of his fingers, surprisingly bony. They were both here even if half a lifetime had gone by.

'We don't want to be overheard.' He got up to close the door.

She could not just sit there waiting. She got up to stop him. A closed door seen by the servants would be fatal. She didn't want to spoil everything, she wanted to dwell on her new-found past until it began to feel real.

They struggled entangled as if sewn together with his arms in her sleeves.

'You're out of your mind.'

'We have an account to settle,' he said. 'It's been too long. You owe me too much. As much as I owe you.'

At these words all her sorrows welled up to block the throat. He manœuvred her to the divan and pushed her on to it. The clasp of her ear-ring cut into the side of her face. The round thick rosewood border of a marble panel thrust up hard against the back of her head. There was no time, there never was any. The ever-watchful scheme of things could make animals of men and girls who were alone at last for a minute, as in the old romances. It had to happen instantly or not at all. Especially with them, unless he took her now there could be no arrangements to meet in a safer place. There were just too many things between them that no amount of words could clear away.

Still she fought him, her resistance having found a focus. With the bitterness piled up over the years she would rather give in to any other man than him. They tussled over the trousers sash that left a narrow red line on her, a visible barrier. He squashed her hands with his full weight leaning on one side, his elbow hurting her as he arched up to pull down his trousers. She could sense the danger outside the room, tremendous pressure on a bubble. Their struggle seemed enclosed in a glass dome much smaller

129

than the room. People could see through. Perhaps even he was looking. Her wrist was pressed against the fur lining of his gown on the couch. The feel of fur touched off that fear of mating like animals and a sudden spurt of madman's strength. She threw him off and got on her feet and only then heard voices outside. He was also listening sitting up. A trap she thought. It sounded like people arguing. She rushed to open the door hoping that nobody had seen it shut. On the way she straightened her clothes and hair a bit. At least there was no one outside in the ill-lit hall. That was Wong Ji's voice remonstrating at the back door outside the kitchen, the only entrance in use.

'What is it, Wong Ji?' she called out.

'Some people here asking for Third Master.'

Two men came into the hallway wearing black satin caps more pointed than usual and black gaberdine gowns with salt-like snow on the shoulders.

'Is this the lady of the house?' one of them turned around to ask Wong Ji who followed close behind.

'How could you be such a fool, Wong Ji, to let in strangers at night?' she said.

'I kept telling them to wait outside——'

'Mistress, please ask Third Master to come out, we came with Third Master,' the men said.

'People you don't know, you let them force their way in?' she insisted on speaking only to Wong Ji. 'End of the year and you're not more careful of doors and windows?' There were more robberies when people needed money for the New Year.

'Here's Third Master,' cried the men when he came out of the parlour. 'Huh-ya, Third Master, you certainly kept us waiting. In this snow too.' 'We're frozen stiff and footsore, one at the back door, one at the front door, didn't dare leave our posts either, and no dinner.' 'Huh-ya, we thought you'd left by another door. Worried to death what to tell the others when we get back.'

'You people wait outside,' he took them by the arms and started to walk them towards the door. 'Wait outside, I'll be with you in a minute. Go get rickshas, you can wait in the rickshas.'

'Now, wouldn't it embarrass Third Master?' they said reproachfully. 'Throw us into the snowstorm just when we've found Third Master at last?'

'Who are these people?' she said to nobody in particular.

'We came with Third Master, Mistress. Third Master has a bill to settle with us, and with Mr Ung here from the Yuan Feng Money Shop.'

Mr Ung said, 'We're hard-pressed for money ourselves, end of the year. We went to Third Master's residence and were told he was out. So what could we do but wait? We camped in the parlour with the other collectors and slept on the floor. It's been weeks now. Third Master came downstairs today and promised to go out and raise money. The others had the two of us go along with him.'

'All right,' he cut in, 'now you know I didn't give you the slip. This is not my house, you can't make a row here. Just walk ahead of me, I'll be right with you.'

'Please don't make things difficult for us, Third Master. If we go, we go together.'

'Ours is a hardship post and Third Master has always been most considerate,' said the other.

'Everybody out,' she said. 'Pushing into people's houses at night—who knows what you are? If you still won't go we'll call the police.'

'Get out, get out,' Wong Ji murmured pushing at the men. 'Our mistress has spoken.'

Third Master herded them on whispering while they begged, 'Third Master is most understanding, he knows the fix we're in. If we go back alone they'll think we got some special consideration from Third Master. And how are we going to account for ourselves back at the shop?'

She cut them short, 'Go talk business elsewhere, this is not a tea house. We don't owe you money here, what right have you got to barge in at all hours? Wong Ji, go call the police.'

'Second Sister-in-law,' he turned to her for the first time and she slapped him hard. He started to hit back but Wong Ji caught hold of his arm pleading under his breath, 'Third Master. Third Master.'

The bewildered creditors also held him back babbling, 'All right, all right, Third Master, it's all among ourselves, there's nothing that can't be talked over.'

He looked across them at her. 'All right, you be careful. Just be careful, or you'll have me to reckon with.'

He walked out with the two men at his heels and Wong Ji behind them. She went back to the parlour. She did not want to go up just now with all the amahs upstairs. Wong Ji would not come in here. The lights were curiously bright. The flowers' fragrance mingled with cigarette smoke as after a party. She didn't go near the stove. There was a faint hum inside it, the sound of burning timber breaking off and falling. The little window on the stove looked into an empty red room.

For the want of something to do she uncorked the bottle that he was to take with him and took a sip. All the dried roses crowding on the surface almost stopped the flow. It was slightly rasping and tasted bitter. The sugar was all at the bottom. The gongs and drums were still beating far off warming up the New Year.

12

The sixtieth birthday of Big Master Gunglin of the old second branch was to be celebrated with a private performance of Peking opera by famous singers. Mostly only big gangsters had birthday parties like this nowadays. In their set such displays would seem out of place after the fall of the empire even if it was already twenty years after. They were people who had lost their country, so to speak, finding shelter in the foreign settlements. Their land in the interior was exposed to the civil wars. A common subject of conversation when they met was the difficulty of collecting ground rents. Going into business was too risky without experience. Nothing was quite worth it after officialdom where 'capital and profit are one to ten thousand', according to the old saying. Government jobs were out of the question. It would be collaborating with the enemy, disgracing the family. They were in fact all in the same position as Yindi, as she had put it, a widow living on some dead money. The rich ones did not show off on birthdays either. Ninth Old Master went to the West Lake in Hangchow every year to avoid his birthday.

The Yaos and their relatives spoke of the coming event with a sour little smile, slightly embarrassed.

'The old master is in such good spirits.'

'They say it's the sons who insisted.'

'It's always supposed to be the sons' idea.'

'Are you going?'

'Well, got to be there cheering.'

Nobody would miss it. Two of the four great female impersonators were coming down specially from Peking with their own retinues and would make no trouble about

133

the billing on the scarlet programme sheet. The gas-lit stage was set in the courtyard that was covered for the occasion by mat roofing. The seats extended on to the porches. The women sat in the balcony that ran around three sides of the courtyard with stringed bulbs on the handrails, a necklace around all the faces, the pretty ones leaping to the eye. Yindi was lost in the fashionable crowd. At just over forty, she dressed like an old lady in a baggy dark silk gown with a few pieces of inconspicuous jewellery so that nobody could comment in any way. But she made up for it with loud greetings and observations in a matter-of-fact manner, unsmiling.

'So the gowns are long again, but sleeves are getting shorter and shorter. A couple of years ago the knees were out, now it's the elbows. Always getting longer or shorter, never any peace. Can you wonder at all the wars? One day when gowns and sleeves are neither long nor short, there'll be law and order in the world.'

'How do you think of such things?' Second Mistress Sun said laughing with an abstracted look behind the eyes that Yindi had come to recognize. Her remarks were being committed to memory to make the rounds, yet another famous joke to be recalled and pondered every time there was a fresh upheaval and change of government, wondering if this could be the millennium, for in a way they believed in her. And she did not mind any more.

Watching the show she pulled her niece's pigtail. Big Master's elder daughter was talking to the girl in front with elbows planted on the other's chair back.

'Ai-yo, Miss, why have you lost so much hair? Your pigtail used to be a handful. Why, the young lady must be pining for her in-laws.'

The girl blushed and grabbed back her pigtail. 'Second Aunt is always like this.'

'We must send word to the Yangs to hurry up with the wedding.'

'Really, Second Aunt!' She jerked around to face the other side holding her hair.

'Good for you, you didn't cut your hair. Most girls have,' said Second Mistress Sun.

'The Yangs probably won't let her,' Yindi said. 'Our Big Mistress herself has cut her hair.'

'It saves trouble to cut it short,' said Second Mistress Sun.

The girl had got up and moved to another row.

'Really, you!' Second Mistress Sun whispered half laughing. 'Even when I kept interrupting.'

'Miss pretends to be angry but she's grateful to me at heart. What's the sense of long engagements? "The cat gets thin from yowling, the fish gets high from hanging." '

'You're worse than ever,' giggled Second Mistress Sun. 'Presuming on your age.'

'Well, "The old should be gay, the young should be steady." '

'So her brother is going abroad,' Second Mistress Sun went on interrupting.

'Everybody wants to go abroad nowadays. With our Yensheng it's not that I can't bear to have him sentenced to exile. In times like these even if you come out first in the foreign imperial examination, you'd still be sitting home when you're back. Of course it's different if you have a rich father.' The word 'rich' had come to stand for 'influential' in their circles. As it was not nice to say that somebody had become an official they would just say lightly, 'So-and-so has got rich.' Not long ago Big Master had 'come out of the mountains', that is, come out of retirement, to take a post in the Nationalist government. There were already a few relatives who had joined the war lords' governments in the north but he was the first among the Yaos.

'You'd never let your Yensheng go,' Second Mistress Sun murmured smiling, afraid of being overheard talking about Big Master. She was a timid soul. When she was with Big Mistress or Third Mistress she would look guilty if she so much as said, 'I played mahjong with your Second Mistress the other day,' for fear they would think gossip had been passed on to the most vicious tongue.

'Have you seen Big Mistress?'

'She's sitting over there.'

'Is Big Master here?'

They dropped their voices at the very mention of him.

'Probably not yet. Look, there's Pink Cloud,' said Second Mistress Sun.

The actress was walking past the front row followed by her train of admirers, turning to nod at friends in the audience. She wore a man's gown and an English checked cap at a rakish angle. A pigtail hung down her back. The footlights alongside shone brightly on the vermilion mouth and round silver face.

'Is that the one that was on just now? Look at that big pigtail—like the young men when we were young. Is that the fifth son of the house behind her?'

'Yes, they say he quarrelled with today's manager to put her number further back.'

'No wonder they say it was the sons that wanted this show—with all the famous names to help boost her. Before it was female impersonators, now it's females. Still they have to get themselves up to look like neither man nor woman.'

She saw her son down below. It was always a shock to see from afar someone right in front of you all day long, as if the proportion was wrong. As he pushed past the row of seats in his black silk box jacket worn over the blue gown he dipped his head in apologetic little bows like an old man's doddering nods. Actually he was well-made, pale with gold-rimmed glasses on a high nose and poised as small men often were, just more old-fashioned than his cousins. They were the worst, always laughing at him. Relatives also wondered why he alone was so small and thin in a tall family. They blamed it on her salty food. She had to save even in the days of Old Mistress in order to squeeze the money for opium out of their allowances, mother and son dining in their rooms on pickles, salted vegetables and salted fish which stunted his growth, dried him up and choked him so he got asthma. She was furious when she heard this. Asthma he'd had from birth, got it from his father. They forgot how small Second Master had been, they had been conditioned to forget him even when he was alive. Old Mistress had been short too and so was Ninth Old Master the grand-uncle.

'There's our Yensheng,' she explained her leaning forward to look.

'Ah, yes. A grown man now.' The ruminative tone was faintly disagreeable. Again thinking of his height and diet?

'Twenty already and still a child, afraid of people,' she said.

'That's why it's so ridiculous, the things people make up,' Second Mistress Sun murmured carelessly.

She could hear there were words within words. 'What about?' she asked smiling.

'Such a joke. He was said to have been host at a singsong house party.'

'Oh? Our Yensheng? You should have seen him in front of women. His eyes look at his nose and his nose looks down at his heart.'

'That's why it's such a joke.'

'Where did you hear this?'

'Now who was it that was saying—look at this memory of mine. Somebody was said to have run into Third Master one day—' She looked away as she spoke the name but Yindi knew she was being closely watched for any change of expression. It was common knowledge that he and she were not speaking. She was said to have slapped his face. There had been a lot of talk. It had to do with a loan, but even then. As to there actually being anything between them, the general opinion was he hadn't come to that yet, his own sister-in-law after all and getting on to forty. She wouldn't dare either.

'And Third Master wanted him to come along because Yensheng was throwing a party for the first time he said, and didn't know enough people to fill the tables.'

'This is still more strange,' she said. 'We haven't seen Third Master for years.'

'I thought it sounded unlikely.'

'How on earth did he think of it, using a child's name as a lure.'

'Well, anything is possible with your Third Master.'

'When was this?'

'Not so long ago, was it?'

'For one thing he never goes out alone.'

'Perhaps it's just as well for a boy to get some experience in the outside world.'

'A fine start if he were to follow in the footsteps of his Third Uncle.'

'At least with an old hand by his side he won't be cheated.'

The joke cut her like a knife. 'Who knows what it was all about really? Did anybody actually see him?'

'I don't think the man went. This kind of talk always goes in my right ear and comes out the left ear. I remember this much only because it's so funny.'

'I just wonder what started this talk.'

'Don't take it seriously or I'd blame myself for telling you.'

'How is Third Master doing?'

'I don't know, haven't heard.'

'Is Third Mistress here?'

'I haven't seen her.'

'Third Mistress is pitiful now.'

'She's all right,' the other whispered. 'Some peace and quiet at last as I told her.'

'Have you been to her new house?'

'Yes, it's small but she doesn't need much room all by herself.'

'Third Master never comes?'

'Just as well, although I shouldn't say this.'

'Just left her like that, after so many years of marriage. After all she took for him from Old Mistress.'

'Well, your Third Mistress is a model wife.'

'That's just it, too much of a model. Even I can't stand it looking on.'

With their conversation safely back in the old groove they both felt this was the right moment to stop and turn back to the stage. First she looked for Yensheng. He wasn't where she had just seen him. She looked all over the court-yard underneath feeling suddenly lost. Come to think of it he had been going to the Chans lately to listen to in-terpretations of Buddhist classics. Old Mr Chan had been a mandarin once and had taken up Buddhism now that he was half paralysed. He formed a Society of Buddhist Studies and put out little books. Yensheng sometimes brought one home. The old man smoked opium and was a late riser. The sessions often ended after midnight. No wonder. . . .

Third Master was not down there either. The last few

years relatives had seen to it that she was never in the same room with him because they were not on speaking terms. But Yensheng could have run into him among the men guests. They must have slipped away together and Yensheng came back to the party later. The women upstairs wouldn't know, like today. That was what shook her most, the two of them getting together turning against her. If he had come to her, although she wouldn't even see him it would still be different. Could it be just his idea of a joke? Taking her son out? He used to be given to these pranks. But she dismissed the idea instantly almost as a fresh outrage.

Last time it was her own fault to have hit him in front of people. Of course the talk had got out. Fortunately everybody lived apart these days and the eldest branch wanted as little to do with the other two as possible. After all this was not like the case in Nanking where their Cousin Fung lived openly with a widowed sister-in-law and used her money, with his wife in the same house. The fact was that she sat home by herself year in and year out, her servants and warders could bear witness. And it was not as if she had anybody else, then it would have been within his rights as brother-in-law to catch her as he had threatened when he walked out of her house. As it was, her only fear was that he might sink so low he would get on heroin and come for money, and when he was not let in would shout outside the door, capable of saying anything and carry on for days, sleeping in the alley. There was also one like this among their relatives.

She heard he had got rid of one of his concubines. Then it turned out there was a new one installed on Medhurst Road.

'This one has money,' people snickered.

'Is Third Master using her money?' she would ask.

'With these singsong girls, if they just share expenses it's rare enough.'

'What does she look like?'

'Nothing much, they say.'

'How old?'

'Old. Retired twice already.'

'Well, they say those that know how to play around prefer old ones.' She made a point of joking freely when he was mentioned.

So he had found somebody with money. And it couldn't have been all because of money in spite of the uncomplimentary things they said. Only men had been to his place and they never spoke well of other men's concubines lest they seemed covetous. This had proved something to her and actually made her feel a little better.

But how hard these singsong girls were, and at this age they were the mosquitoes that have lived on to the autumn, with a real bite to their sting. If the woman was not openhanded he would still have to scrounge around for money. And there was still the other concubine to support. He had left his wife for good and relatives saw very little of him. She could imagine, when one contact after another had been used for the last time, his thoughts would turn to her again, just as she kept thinking of him, coldly but always going back. She felt it now, the chill dead weight creeping up pulling her along, endless, two big snakes half-heartedly wringing each other to death.

Did he tell Yensheng? He wouldn't since he hadn't all along. But you can't tell, now that he is getting old and down and out he may want to brag. Surely it's not a good way to make friends, to say things about a man's mother? What can't you say in a singsong house? Trying to make him stay a little longer at night, 'What are you afraid of? She's a good one herself.' She had not noticed any change in Yensheng's manner lately. Was he so deep? He was his father's son. She never could tell how much Second Master had guessed why she hanged herself.

'Ugh!' an abrupt cry from the back rows downstairs. The cheers said *how*, good, compressed into the half-strangled *ugh*.

Here it was back again, that day in the temple. She never knew she had to go through that again, that bursting bottled-in loneliness of being in a crowd out of key with the tumult inside her, the innards all shaken and scrambled and the feet melted away, no ground to stand on. Where did he get the money? He didn't learn to borrow against his inheritance? With that familiar clause, 'Wait for the end of Mother's natural years.' But she was not Old Mistress's age, nor was the family known for being rich as before. Had he stolen anything? Not jewellery; she had opened the jewellery box today when she was dressing and did not notice anything missing. But land and house deeds?

'Ugh! Ugh!' up went the cheers.

She could not leave early. Some men never stayed long, it was understood that they had to go home to smoke opium, but there was no excuse for women. Besides she wouldn't want Second Mistress Sun to see her go in a hurry.

Dinner was late and took for ever, then back to the opera. She sat far away from Second Mistress Sun and soon got up to find the hostesses to take her leave. The amah she brought went down to look for Yensheng. She was gone a long time and came back to say that the servants of the house could not find him.

'We're going, we won't wait for him,' she said.

The men downstairs called rickshas for her. Now that cars became more common, private rickshas were out of fashion. She did not need one at the house anyway and those ricksha pullers were the worst, teaching the young masters bad ways. A couple of years ago when Yensheng went out she used to have a servant go with him. But this was not done nowadays and she had to let him go about alone like the other boys, so now this.

Once home she checked the papers in a rosewood box she kept locked in the bureau. The antiques, silver, paintings and calligraphies were all packed in trunks on the top floor, too late to open them tonight. He was bound to be back in the middle of it. Seeing them may put ideas in his head. Besides it was no use her looking. Dealers had to be called in to check them against lists to see if fakes had been substituted. There were people on hand who could teach him such tricks.

She questioned the servants separately. They all said they knew nothing about it. Of course they were afraid of trouble, especially to come between mother and son. When the thing blew over it would be the servants who would get the blame. What was more, she knew these people were listless under the austerities of these years with her. They wouldn't dare show it but they wouldn't put themselves out. They had learned to get by merely keeping out of her way.

She would come back to them another day. She searched his room herself and found nothing. There was the stack of movie synopses he collected, standing three feet high. He always took a pile every time, it was free and beautifully printed on glossy paper. He like Douglas Fairbanks and Vilma Banky with her yellow hair worn in a bun like a Chinese, billed simply as Miss Banky or Miss Pung Kai, the only actress thus honoured because she looked so lady-like—so unlike his mother, she sometimes suspected, that was why he liked her. He always sat at the end of a row near the exit in case of fire. This was so unlike him, entirely because somebody else put him up to it, like the Emperor Kwang Hsu turning against the Dowager Empress, all the more hateful for being a puppet. Fire blew out of her eyes when she saw him walk in.

'How is it Mother came back first? Feeling all right?' He sat down pretending to be calm.

'Where did you go?' she began casually enough, lying on the couch.

'The show is just finished. How is it you didn't stay till the end?'

'Looked everywhere and couldn't find you. Where did you run off to?'

'I was there. Unless I was backstage watching them make up.'

'Still lying, taking everybody else for dead, running off all the time mucking around. Buddhist sermons indeed—make them up as you go, just paper houses pasted together to cheat the dead.' She shouted him down so he stopped speaking.

'Say where you went. Speak.' She sat up. 'Come here. I'm asking you. Where did you go? Good examples you don't follow, you learn from your Third Uncle. Is he somebody you can mess around with? He hates me because of borrowing money. Now he wants you to make me die of anger and you're fool enough to do it?'

He just sat there saying nothing. She suddenly ran over and pulled out thirty-odd dollars from his pocket.

'Where did you get this? Speak.'

She finally slapped him left and right as if questioning a thief. He was so angry he blurted out, 'Third Uncle lent me.' He knew this hurt most.

'Good, your Third Uncle has money. You go and be his son. If you're going to be like him I'd rather have you dead. Beat you to death, beat you to death——' She hit

144

him on the head and face. 'How much did you take from him? It's easy money to use?'

Backing and parrying he started to hit back, at which Old Cheng appeared by his side pulling at his arms dragging him away. 'Ek, Young Master! It's late, Mistress, ask him tomorrow. Young Master has always been timid, he's probably too frightened to speak, he's never seen Mistress in such a temper.'

It was a way out. She let Old Cheng push him out of the room and put him to bed. Sons so big do not get beatings except with a plank administered in the ancestral temple in the presence of elders of the clan. But not for a thing like this. The whole world is on the side of the young man stepping out.

She had him closely watched and spoke to him again the next day, wept and made scenes invoking motherhood and widowhood. But no matter how she was nice to him one day and bad the next, she never got another word out of him. He had the air of waiting it out. If she locked him up she would not be able to keep it up for long. Relatives would blame her first off for not getting him a wife before this. Boys were at large the minute they were finished with the schoolroom. His old tutor had left last year. Without imperial examinations the study of the classics was a long weary road without landmarks, generally terminated by marriage.

But people were marrying later. His cousins of the eldest branch were drifting around with nothing to do, taking lessons in German and tennis, counterparts to their sisters' French and piano playing. Before their father's defection they were talking of going to high school at their age, a missionary school, less disloyal than government-run schools. Other families more on the fringe were less discriminating about schools and colleges. Some boys even worked in government banks. It was supposed to matter less with the younger generation, that much further away from their ancestors. The news was broken in an offhand way half defiantly to nonplussed recipients who could only answer faintly, 'Oh, good. Banks are good,' or 'Good to go to college.' Those that could afford it got round the rule by sending their sons abroad or to British Hong Kong for schooling. Even girls went to school in the last couple of years, at least the younger ones. Hers was about the only household that adhered strictly to the unspoken tradition. Yensheng filled his father's place and lay low, 'doused the light and nurtured darkness' like all the older men. It suited her. She knew it would be a losing business one way or another for him to go out into the world. It was not that she didn't think him intelligent enough—just innate motherly pessimism, as common and incurable as a mother's optimism. She still believed that her son would be different. He could stay at home like the older genera- tion without their other side, the women and gambling that made up for the uneventfulness of their lives and in- variably got out of hand. She had never realized before the irresistible pressure of the vacuum, what amounted to the force of life itself.

All she knew about the singsong houses were the con- cubines that came out of there, some not even pretty. They seemed to lose their powers once they were out of the light of that world, so inaccessible to her it was almost beyond jealousy. They not only ruined Third Master but left him childless. Practically all singsong girls were barren, maybe because of the abortion herbs that their madams had forced on them too often. And he devoted his life to them, the one legitimate source of love and romance and as vast as the sea, overwhelming by the sheer force of their num- bers. They got him into the habit of 'looking into the pot

146

while eating from the bowl', as the saying goes. With her he had never been all there. And now little as she had they were going to take it too.

13

She called in matchmakers.

'His wife will keep an eye on him, I can't any more.'

It was understood that he had to make a suitable marriage. It was the only way they could make use of the family background—the only honourable way, not like getting into new governments on the strength of being a Yao. But when it came to the point nobody seemed to want to give his daughter to the Yaos' second branch, the father a freak, the mother from the lower classes and known to be fierce. It would not have mattered if he was the son of a concubine, who had to be self-effacing while this one would be a regular mother-in-law. They were said to have money, but did not look it. The matchmakers had to go farther afield to the interior to get them a photograph from the Fungs of Wuweichow, distant relatives. When the family was right they could not be too choosy about looks.

'Such a big mouth,' Yensheng said but did not object strongly which was taken as consent, as was the custom. Marriage should make him a man and set him free. His mother was already more agreeable since the talks started with the Fungs. He also wanted to humour her.

'Roll me a pill,' she said. 'That stupid slave girl will never learn. You used to play at it when you were little.'

'I liked the tools.' He twiddled the long needle and the little shield with cut-out designs.

He lay down and fixed her a pipe that puffed and hissed straight to the end.

'Not stuck once,' she said, 'and that was a large one too.

The thing is to make it an even brown and loose-knit. You must have had practice in the singsong houses.'

It was the first time she had spoken tolerantly of his outings. He murmured no, half laughing and made her another.

'You have this one,' she said. 'It's fun as long as it doesn't get to be a habit. When you were a sick baby you used to have smoke blown in your face.'

He took it and put-putted away like a little train.

'You must have smoked outside.'

'No, I didn't.'

'Play is play, all right in its place, but don't go out just now, wait till we've settled this with the Fungs. You're still so young, they will say.'

No wonder people talked business on the opium couch in singsong houses; it put you in a nocturnal mood, relaxed and intimate around the little lamp. But what did he care how his suit went?

She seemed to read his thoughts. 'What I like about the Fungs is they are old-fashioned, not like the girls of today—heaven help us if we get one of those in the house. Also you might say the family has roots. Your Aunt Chu has seen the girl, so it can't go far wrong. You want a beauty, wait until the important business is out of the way. Even I won't have you unhappy. You're all I have.'

Other parents had struck this bargain with their sons to make them go through with a marriage. Coming from his mother it was still a surprise. Only a gleam at the edge of his glasses betrayed his unseemly joy.

'As long as you choose well. Just don't be a garbage cart like your uncles. Your Third Uncle has ruined his own signboard, it doesn't give you face to be seen with him. You never can tell when a person is desperate, he may take his cut behind your back, maybe on your girl too.

These singsong houses, once they take you for a fool, they can let you hang around forever getting your appetite up.'

A controlled expression on his face gave her the feeling that may be exactly what happened. If he had got a taste of it his heart would have flowered as a bean might sprout. It is a madness, especially at first. He wouldn't be so quiet after being kept home for days, nor would he be so sensitive to mere tenderness from a woman. The little oil lamp shone brighter than any other, being seen lying down from a fresh angle of the eye. The face beyond the light revolted her slightly. There was something monstrous about a face grown unrecognizable over the years, but she was not the young mother he remembered either. They felt so safe together, a little sad too at the reunion. For a moment she was close to tears, willing to live her life through him. He was a part of her and male.

He was looking at her with a curious smile that made his face pathetically thin. He had never expected anything from her in all his life but now she loved him. She did not like it, as if he had his hand on a soft spot on her. Right away she was angry. Even her own son—the minute she got affectionate it meant a great outlay of money. It made no difference that the suggestion had come from herself.

She changed the subject, back to the usual topic of relatives to make him talk. He had a turn for wry sarcasm that showed only when he was talking to her.

'Was Big Master there that day?' They were still speaking of the birthday party.

'Just put in an appearance.'

Even in their own home voices automatically dropped to a whisper with a sense of the sinister and some awe.

'Was Ma Chifang there?' in the same hushed tone. Peripheral relatives were referred to by their full names with a hint of contempt. This was Big Master's brother-in-law, the head of the secretariat of the war lord Wu Peifu, now back in Shanghai after Wu's downfall.

'He never goes out. Somebody went to see him and was told Master was not well.'

'That's why how can you tell about things nowadays.'

'Well, he just printed a collection of his poems. Sent us a copy too. He was the ghostwriter of Old Wu's bad poems.'

'What a coincidence, these two brothers-in-law. It has to be all in their branch.' And it had to be Big Master, the only likely son, the one Old Mistress had leaned on, the only one that could possibly be said to remind people of his grandfather.

' "The poet Ma Chifang" he's called. It makes your flesh creep the way he flatters Old Wu, the wise lord, the scholarly general.'

'The Mas have always been shameless, the way they made up to your family. It's different for Big Master. That's where Old Mistress was really blessed, not to have lived to see it.'

'It wouldn't have happened if Old Mistress was alive.'

'Who was it that was still speaking for him the other day?—said "He was a district governor originally." So he was a mandarin in his own right, he has the seniority any time he cares to come out again and owes nothing to his ancestors.'

'He probably had no choice. Said to be in terrible straits,' he said in his confidential elderly manner.

'With his way of spending,' she grunted. She had always said the two brothers were just as bad but she did not want to bring up Third Master again so soon. Big Master had taken more trouble covering up in his mother's days. Having stuck it out he had simply spread out in all directions. How else would he have come to this within a few years of the division of property? However the subject of inheritance was never mentioned to Yensheng.

'So Little Feng is going abroad,' he said enviously.

'Just don't bring a foreign wife back. I wonder Big Mistress is not worried. People make them marry before they go.'

'They'd just want a divorce when they come back. Take off trousers to fart—why bother?'

'At least he's not sending Little Pu abroad, much as he likes him.' It was just like Big Master to adopt a clansman's son, when he had sons himself. To show the old clan spirit, and it happened that his grandfather had also adopted a son from the clan when there was a son and heir already.

'Can't do without him,' said Yensheng.

'They say Little Pu is bad.' So was Second Old Master, the other adopted son. As a mandarin he had been known for wanting money. As an ambassador he had brought back a French concubine to add to his large collection. So far Little Pu was only going with singsong girls, no mean feat for a poor young man who was short and fat to boot with a greasy dark complexion and a grumpy furtive look. Of course he must be making some money out of the errands he ran. He hung around the favourite concubine's house, the *de facto* official residence. Big Mistress sometimes did not get to see the master for days, then Little Pu would bring a message. 'Big Mistress just can't stand him.' How like Big Master to take on somebody like that just for the feudal sense of patronage and power and the imagined devotion of the runt everybody disliked. Even Third Master was more sensible there and got more out of his money.

'He managed to get on the good side of the concubine.'

'Yes, it wouldn't do either if he's too handsome.' She opened the seamless little silvery box shaped like a flat seal stood on end, dipped the needle in the thick black liquid and held the tip over the flame. 'The Wong sisters were the belles that day, dressed like twins,' she went back to the birthday. 'Did you see?'

'I saw,' he mumbled boredly. They were his prettiest cousins and laughed at people more than any of the others. The very mention of Second Aunt and Cousin Yensheng and they collapsed backwards and forwards laughing.

'These two—no father, no mother, live with an aunt so they'd have somebody to look after them. Even if the widow lady doesn't benefit by it you'd think at least she'd save a little. Huh! Always squealing for Aunt to stand them treats. And Sixth Mistress Wong is pitiful now, really has to pinch and save. She's supposed to keep the young ladies company in sewing, embroidering and going out, keep an eye on them. Of course it's Aunt who pays at theatres and restaurants, can't let the children pay. Small advantages mean a lot to these rich girls. When boy friends give them presents, the more expensive the more they like it. The boys are willing to invest too and poor Sixth Mistress Wong dies of fright. Just shocking goings on she says.'

'As if that lady can control them,' he snickered blushing.

'Such skinflints already at their age and always sneering at people—not a sign of longevity, although I shouldn't say this. Both their parents died of tuberculosis. They all have it.'

'They do?' He sounded shaken.

'Why not? Only they don't like to mention it. In all fairness though, but for this illness in the family they wouldn't be so well off either. That's why they're the only Wongs that have money. Their father didn't get to spend it. They said our second branch has no man. We're lucky to have no man.'

They had one now. It struck her the minute the words were out of her mouth but he didn't seem to notice. He was still in a rosy glow, shy and happy.

'Second Master Liu is a bank manager now,' he said.

'He must have put money in.' Shanghai was a jungle for those with a little money to invest. It was retribution in a way, that these men should become as hemmed in as she. Some held it in for years before they burst out in a gambling binge, a new woman or business venture, then lay low apparently for good.

'He made a bit on stocks.'

'He has money,' she grunted in a tone of dismissal.

'The Chans still live on Bubbling Well Road?'

'Yes. Their eldest is said to like to dance.'

'What do the Chans live on nowadays?'

'Their mother has money,' she grunted.

It was enough just to mention a name to make you smile. Each was well set up in his own niche in the catacombs. Any news from them was always a surprise and good for a laugh. The relatives had become mutually dependent there, with an instant quickening as the word went round, the only blood circulation in their system. It was reassuring to know that life was still going on elsewhere, at other people's peril. The sense of foreboding made it rain outside, dark grey in the windows and cosier than ever around the little lamp at eye-level. He had learned all these names and kinships from her ever since he was little. The roll-call never got to his father or her family. He had no parents and she had no past but they never felt it, their world was so full and self-sufficient.

'Their Little Fifth has his eyes on Pink Cloud,' he said grinning, back to the birthday performance.

'I saw them together after she got out of costume.'

'She's not much to look at offstage.'

'She has a certain dash.'

'Lively enough,' he admitted and hastened to add, 'onstage.'

'Yes, offstage these actresses can be very stiff. Actually they are more strictly brought up than the young ladies nowadays. They're so afraid of their teacher. There's also their parents, usually very old-fashioned, these northern theatre people.'

'They have terrible burdens, the family and their own musicians, their own troupe, scores of people depending on them for a living. How much will it cost Little Fifth to retire Pink Cloud?'

'Little Fifth won't get her. For one thing his father won't let him. Too much in the public eye. They generally end up as gangsters' concubines. Theirs is a sad life too in spite of all the glory. They're grateful when people have real feelings for them. There's this Old Mrs Wang, she's an opera fan. She boosted an actress, paid for her costumes and curtains and adopted her as daughter as the men do, and they say she was very filial, always coming to the house to stay. In the end she became the old lady's son's concubine.'

He reddened. 'Who was that? Did she sing in Shanghai?' And, 'Which Wangs are these?'

The only way to reach inside him was through some girl.

'She was the leading lady at the Great World in Hangchow.'

He half giggled. The Great World was an indoors amusement park in Shanghai. The one in Hangchow must be a still more countrified carnival.

R.N.—L 155

'No, their Peking opera was supposed to be good. She played serious roles. Good-looking they say and good voice.'

'Pink Cloud doesn't have much of a voice.'

'You don't need it for comedy. Besides girls' voices are too sharp and often squeaky. That's why female impersonators are supposed to sing better. But after they become women their voice broadens.'

'About how old is she?' he said after a moment's silence. 'It's not likely that she still needs broadening?'

'Oh, these actresses are so closely watched by their families, you can't judge by the way they go about with the likes of Little Fifth.'

They compared her with all the others. Her waist was not the smallest but it was supple. Her face was too full, you could see how far the false lock of hair in front of the ears was moved forward to cut down the cheek. She looked smart in men's clothes, she would probably do well in turnabout roles. Yindi felt slightly ridiculous standing there adoring shoulder to shoulder, fondly critical, two fatuous faces basking in a distant sun. But it was exciting to tempt him, she could feel the warmth of a young man's desire. She was the first woman in the world as long as she would talk to him about that girl.

She did not really know much about Peking opera. Being a native of Shanghai she had trouble understanding the lyrics and jokes. But the common enemy of the women of her generation were the singsong girls and the songs they sang were from Peking opera. To admire the real singers would be going one better on them. The women on the stage had rouged eyelids continuous with the deep pink cheeks just like she herself when she was young. Their spangled head-dress full at the back and cut into a pointed arch over the forehead reminded her of the pearl cap she used to wear. The comediennes wore the jacket and trousers fashionable about ten years ago, like hers, just flashier and embroidered all over, which looked right over the footlights. The resemblance was so haunting she was easily moved by the story. If it was possible to take such a one into the house, then that glittering world that once she could only eavesdrop on from the veranda in the dark, she could go in at last even if it was only in the role of dowager empress. Like the old lady in *A Dream in the Red Chamber* who likes to be surrounded by beauties and served only by them. Even their own Old Mistress here had had her court made up of her sons' wives and concubines, all chosen for their charms and then relegated to a manless life. It would be different with her son and his famous beauty, they would attend on her like the Golden Boy and White Jade Maid of the Goddess Kwannon, with a mysterious smile between the three of them that came of her knowledge of that love she had brought about and shut away in a room for life. It was as if the bond of flesh and blood had come alive. But she knew it was all make-believe, enough for some women when they were old enough.

'I know you like Pink Cloud,' she said smiling.

'I'm not qualified,' he mumbled smiling.

'There are ways and means too if we really want it. Nothing is easier than meeting them. The thing is to find the right person to talk terms to the parents. For instance Third Master Liu, he goes in for amateur theatricals and knows all the famous actors. And all the actresses want to be known as their pupils. A word from the teacher would mean a lot. Ninth Old Master is a big promoter himself but there's no need to go to him. There's lots of others, people who know theatre owners and those are the gangsters. You have to be, to open a theatre. And it takes a gangster to have a hold on those theatre families.'

To hear her talking gently and reasonably it all sounded very possible. He had no idea what influence they still had. Of course they were richer than she would have him believe. Could it be that she had only kept things from him until he was old enough to know? She was saving up for this one adventure, to buy him love and fame as the owner of a celebrity. Who knows?—if it was understood to be his first and last romance. . . . As long as one has to be a concubine—except in the case of the actress marrying her own accompanist, an ignoble end—of course one prefers to be a young man's concubine, especially when he is from an old family and not a playboy, in fact a virgin. Unfortunately there had to be a wife first, then a decent interval. But endless waiting is a thing you learn to get used to when you are young.

'The trouble is when they're still on the rise the parents won't let them go until they've had a few years' big earnings behind them,' she went on murmuring, spinning her opium dream. At his age he needed a dream to keep him in bounds. Once he got into the opium habit he would have more sense of proportion.

She was not worried about the Fungs hearing about the smoking.

'What of it? We can afford it,' she would tell the go-betweens.

Opium smoking was no longer common among young men, they went in for dancing and cabaret girls now. The Fungs would see that it was a good thing if it kept a man at home. It had not stopped Big Master and Third Master from going out but they were different. For one thing it was easy for them to lay hands on money. An opium smoker with no money for a smoke can think of nothing else. He could get it at the singsong houses but how long could Third Master carry him there? This couch was the only place for it. In time he would get to be like her, concerned only with keeping the hearth fire burning and the lamp alight on the couch. Let him get away, she had the kite string in hand now.

14

From time to time reports came that Yensheng's fiancée was ugly.

'It can't be?' Yindi said. 'These people have wicked mouths. Your Aunt Chu has seen her only a few years back. It's true there's the old saying, girls change eighteen times as they grow. But the photograph looks her age and your aunt says it's a good likeness.'

'The photograph is bad enough,' he said.

'Some people don't photograph well. I've always said we should ask somebody else to go and take a look, but it's hard to find an excuse to go to a town like Wuweichow. And if it's too obvious her family wouldn't let her be seen. If we weren't related they wouldn't even let a photograph fall into people's hands.'

He would make himself ridiculous if he harped on the subject. But it evidently worried him.

'There's no broken engagements in our family,' she said. 'Theirs is not a family to trifle with either. The only thing to do is still to try and get somebody to find out more. How are we going to word it, to break with a young lady for no reason that you could name? People will think the worst. It will ruin a girl.'

As their side had originally stipulated for a short engagement, the marriage took place in due course in less than a year. The modern 'civilized weddings' as they were called, were staged in hotel restaurants with bridesmaids and best man and foreign bridal gown and veil in funereal white or pink as a compromise. Yindi was ready to go along with it but the civil ceremony requires a witness and an elder to sponsor the union. Both have to be men of distinction

160

if the families involved want face. Ever since she had trouble matchmaking for her son she had seen through all these relatives and family friends. She did not want to go around begging favours for a thing like this. So it was going to be an old-fashioned wedding which would also dispense with the hired hall. The custom now was to serve cakes and soft drinks after the ceremonies, followed by a Chinese feast in another restaurant, then home to kotow to ancestors and elders in private, with some of the guests returning later for the teasing, 'the row in the bridal chamber'. Since they were starting in the middle with the rituals at home, most of the guests would be there.

'An old-fashioned wedding!' the women had said smiling. 'Why, you seldom get to see one nowadays.'

She put it all on the bride's family. 'They want it. They still go by the old rules.'

She did not overdo it, put on a show of antiquities for their amusement, for it was that, even in the nostalgic women who murmured when children laughed, 'Yes, it was all like this before,' with a curious smile. It was like before but funny, countrified now, mocking their most important memories.

She had toned down everything, just an occasional silk sash draped around the house and over the doors, scarlet crossing bright green, the ends gathered and tucked into hydrangea balls. A red one was worn by the groom over one shoulder. This and the black satin skull cap were the only things that distinguished him from the other men, all in black jackets and blue gowns. He looked sheepish milling around mingling, and often pulled at the sash smiling down at it quizzically.

'Not here yet,' the guests took turns whispering with a half frown, half smile. They had run out of things to say and there was nowhere to sit in the cavernous under-furnished rooms.

'Have to wait for the auspicious hour,' said another.

'It's time now.'

'It must be the flowered sedan-chair is too busy. Today is an auspicious day, so many weddings it was hard to rent one. They're rare now. This one is from the Old City.'

'It's not so far from the Old City to the hotel.'

The bride's party was staying in a hotel.

'Not here yet!'

Finally there were tense low cries, 'It's here, it's here.' The children rushed out and everybody else pressed forward. A string of firecrackers was set off outside the front door, never used before this. He hung back, so did his mother who had just come downstairs, smiling and self-effacing. There was no music, she would have none of that flute band that did for both weddings and funerals and sounded rather like the bagpipes that foreign soldiers march to.

Out of the crowd there was at last a glimpse of the bride in scarlet, blinded by the red kerchief over her head and face, helped by the two hired matrons of joy. The figure seemed rather willowy in the close-fitting short jacket and long skirt of embroidered red silk. The square of scarlet cloth flung over the head dated from more primitive times. The cheap dye came out thinner and darker than the red suit. Just the size of a small tablecloth, it jutted out stiffly somewhere beneath the chin making a monstrous hatchet profile. It made him more nervous.

After they had kotowed to heaven and earth and ancestors they were taken to the bridal chamber and the bride was seated on the bed. Nowadays people object to the wedding chamber all in scarlet, like a red sea they say; the glare is dizzying. So this room looked very ordinary with a four-poster and a mosquito net. The only hint of joy was the stack of new padded blankets along the wall inside the bed with their shiny pink and light green silk facings. The colours somehow struck a chill against the raw cold of the house and the dinginess.

He was dragged over to the bed. An older cousin's wife handed him a scales stick to lift the cloth off her head. He pretended not to know what to do with it and finally complied as a joke. There was an audible gasp in the crowd, mostly children. The unveiled face looking down weighted by the phoenix crown had slit eyes and no chin under the big lips. He barely glanced at her and was about to pass the stick back to the older women and walk away unconcerned.

'Hey, toss the kerchief to the top of the bed!' said the woman. 'Toss it high now. Top of the bed.'

He pitched it up with a wave of the stick and made his escape but the bride remained on display the rest of the day holding her pose with bowed head. At the feast she was placed at the head of the table with him, still im-immobile. Afterwards she was moved back again to the bed. The two matrons of joy kept things going. Despite their neat servant-like appearance they had to be good-looking as well as quick-tongued in their profession to draw fire away from a pretty bride, and when the bride was un-attractive the men could tease them instead. Very few people stayed tonight for the row in the chamber. The mother-in-law was not supposed to be present at the 'row' and was seen only briefly earlier at the edge of the crowd in the doorway.

She said as soon as she had a moment alone with her son, 'Ai-ya, how is the bride so ugly? What to do? What to do?'

The bride came to her the next morning and spoke in a low hoarse voice like a man with a cold.

'As if reared on cornhusk,' she said behind her back.

'Well, you've seen our bride,' she said to relatives. 'Chop up her lips and they'll make a heaping dish.'

Yensheng took it coolly. Anyway it was just a duty that he owed his family. Of course it was a hard blow. He was always made to feel he was not as good as the others ever since he was little, and now this. His mother was to blame, but the presence of the intruder drew them even closer together. There were whispered consultations on the opium couch like emergency meetings, except that they were still able to laugh. He was the privileged observer in the clan war with the Fungs of Wuweichow who had bested them in a bargain, or the reporter covering a war between two provinces both keen on good public relations, giving him all facilities at the front. Where he had been reticent about the singsong girls, his present anxiety to dissociate himself from the ugly newcomer loosened his tongue.

The bride was not entirely unaware of what went on behind her back. She came in every morning with the single word of greeting, 'Mother,' gruff and unsmiling. She wore a low S-shaped chignon and a wispy fringe and the fashions of a few years ago, the short blouse and long gathered skirt of the same thin wool in faint plaids of neutral colours. They looked quite smart on her. She powdered heavily over her freckles with just a dab of lipstick to the centre of the mouth. She had the plain girl's defensive calm and seemed to assume her duties in the house matter-of-factly, which annoyed Yindi very much.

'Never seen such a bride. Like a woman who's been married for years.'

She found fault with her all the time. Thirty years a daughter-in-law, thirty years a mother-in-law, every woman has her turn. Not a day passed without an incident. Yensheng's wife would cry in her room. Sometimes he found himself furtively comforting her. But he would tell his mother in detail what she was like in bed. They were like old girl friends; now that he was married he felt obliged to satisfy the widow's curiosity and could not help boasting a little.

He was beginning to go out again, to keep out of the trouble at home he said. She asked enough questions to feel sure that he had not been seeing Third Master. Still she kept him short. Not cutting much of a figure among the singsong girls he was commendably blasé about them. He did all right in the long run, he could speak Shanghai dialect like the native his mother was and merged into the scene. He kept his head, there was never any talk of taking anybody home. She was proud of him for the first time in his life. He was smarter than his uncles and all the other men. As her representative in enemy territory he did not lose face for her.

'Cousin Yensheng is bad,' now his girl cousins were saying.

'How?'

The other would turn away making a small disgusted noise as if she was not going to answer. 'Whoring, how else?'

Only old people went to singsong houses, or old-fashioned businessmen, so it was not only bad but unfashionable. The next time they saw him they could not help giving him another look and there seemed to be something sinister under his old-fashioned exterior. He stood by the table, small and slight in his dark blue gown, no glasses now, the exquisitely carved face very pale, slick hair parted in the middle, rather like the degenerate rich young men of the interior that they read so much about in modern fiction. He bobbed his head quickly to acknowledge their greetings scarcely glancing their way, in the old approved manner. He waited on his mother with a cynical smile at the back of his eyes. She paid him no attention in front of people, just a muttered order now and then without looking at him, the same as she did towards her daughter-in-law.

It was the lunar New Year. The house buzzed for days with the constant off and on of relatives dropping in to pay their respects. The marcelled girls put on their coats as soon as they had kotowed and warmed their hands under the big fur collars. 'You freeze to death at Second Aunt's,' they complained when they met at other houses.

'Yes, no fire in this weather.'

'People say they warm up leftover cups of lotus seed tea and serve them over and over again. So revolting.'

'I really dread going there. The things Second Aunt says!—just make you die of anger.'

'What was it this time?'

'What else but her kind of talk?' Nothing could make her repeat it.

'Sister-in-law is so pitiful, standing in the hallway peeling lotus seeds, dipping into cold water when the frostbites on her fingers have burst. Why not let the amahs do it, you ask her and she's scared to death, "Mother will be angry." '

Yensheng's wife had to keep her neck down for hours standing in front of the cracked little red bureau. One of the girls got her a chair but could not induce her to sit down. She could be seen from inside the room where Yindi sat on the bed under the parted curtains of dirty white glass cloth. She had been ill and looked small and thin huddled in an old black serge jacket and trousers and spoke faintly, practically inaudible across the room where the guests were seated. Even the iron four-poster looked strangely small standing by itself along the middle of the

166

wall. The servants here also had a way of making themselves scarce. Especially at this time of year with tipping so much in the air they took care not to hang around. It was the custom in some households for the mistress to keep part of the money in the little red packets left on the table.

'Why, what's the matter with you, Second Mistress?' Big Mistress called out in the jocular tone used towards old ladies that may be slightly deaf. 'How come that you weren't well? How so?'

'Hai,' she sighed, 'Big Mistress, this illness of mine all comes from being angry.'

'Why, how is that?' the other pretended not to understand. 'It's not stomach cramps like mine is it? Mine really comes from anger, aches after every meal.' The petite Big Mistress had put on weight, every inch the mandarin's lady all round. Holding office in the monogamous Nationalist government did not reform her husband but at least all his children were hers, that loathsome Little Pu notwithstanding.

'Ah now, what have you got to be angry about, you're blessed.'

'You're the blessed one. But how did you get to be so fragile? How so?'

The relatives had already diagnosed her ailment as the result of that same salty food that had stunted her son's growth. The dishes were salty so it took less to go with the rice. It was mostly hearsay as few had sampled them. For occasions like her son's wedding, cut-rate feasts were ordered from restaurants. Callers were never asked to stay for dinner but once a year on her birthday there was a tea. Everybody who happened upon it was herded over to the ceremonial round table with scarlet tablecloth. She stood leaning across the width of it distributing sweet stuffed buns made to look like peaches and other steamed buns, keeping a grim eye on her chopsticks, not looking at the recipients, grown-ups or children. She had to give them what they were obliged to eat.

This year during the New Year visits some of the older women were pressed to stay for mahjong. It was one of her better days, she felt strong enough to play. Yensheng's wife came in to ask a question woodenly and went out again.

'You can't tell by looking at our young mistress, so stiff and glum,' she said at the mahjong table. 'Huh! the minute she sees Yensheng she has to go sit on the chamber pot.'

There was a flutter of nervous laughter. To prove it she told more about her son and daughter-in-law and got more laughs. 'How did I know? My control doesn't extend to their bed. But these things get out. Men's mouths open wide. When they get together it's all a joke to them. To think that in the days of Old Mistress we were scolded if we so much as mussed our hair a bit coming back from lunch, what with husband and wife eating by themselves in their own room. "Willing to do anything to please a man," was how everybody used to criticize a woman, not just the mother-in-law. So unfair we thought. If the man is not pleased it's your fault again. But how long will it last if the man doesn't respect you? Nowadays it's—really we've never heard the likes before. And we still speak of "families like ours"!'

In time this travelled back to Yensheng's wife's ears. She took it up with him at night, cried and would not let him touch her again. They quarrelled constantly and sometimes fought. This encouraged Yindi to tell people about them at every opportunity.

The story spread gingerly between husband and wife and contemporaries. Two ladies would put their heads together as if whispering about a grave illness. One would suddenly burst into an exasperated snort of laughter and bend forward to nibble the other's ear some more with distaste.

'That's all they like to talk about in their family,' the other would complain.

Yensheng's wife fell ill. At first Yindi said she was pretending. As it dragged on a doctor was summoned who said it was a weakness of breath and deficiency of blood, understood to be tuberculosis.

'When am I going to hold a grandson in my arms with things as they are?' Yindi said. 'We don't want little tubercular demons either. And you ought to have somebody near you, you shouldn't be running out day and night and ruin your health. I'll give you Dungmei, she's grown.'

He had never considered the slave girl, being too used to her as a dirty runny-nosed child. Only recently he had lost his temper at her at dinner.

'Dungmei brought in the soup with her thumbnails in it again,' he cried.

Yindi had suddenly discovered some good in her. 'She's fair-skinned. "Whiteness alone hides three blemishes." Dressed up she will look a different person. A five-shorts figure is lucky for a woman. Short neck, short arms and legs means money and blessings. That big square behind means many sons. It's just borrowing her belly for a son. We need to pour on the joy to thin out all this bad luck. A slave girl "put back in the room" doesn't really count. She won't be called Mistress Concubine. Miss Dung will do. Dungmei to us,' hinting that it would not preclude a serious purchase when there was the money for it. He knew better than to ask. The wars continued. Now it was against the Communists in Kiangsi. The cost of opium soared from the special tax that financed the campaigns. *Prohibition by taxation* was the slogan. Then came downright prohibition and opium went still higher. Smuggling was a government monopoly. The great dark cakes indented in the centre like a rough mortar came with a piece of thin yellow paper pasted over it stamped *For Incineration at Provincial Capital*, in large archaic type like the official papers of the dynasties. The hunk of dark earth had a faint fragrance at its strongest when the sacking was first unwrapped. Cooked in an open pot on a little earthen stove at the head of the staircase it smelled burned, sweet and penetrating. There was a mysterious bustle all over the house as if some Taoist high priest had been asked down to concoct his medicine in seclusion. Nobody ever remarked on the smell but even the servants smiled slightly as they went in and out.

The brew was poured into little brown jars and doled out to the white copper vial, part of the paraphernalia on the tray. Lying face to face with him, eyes riveted to the little light, she sometimes found herself looking at his pipe bowl resting on top of the lamp, just at the hole on the snout of the closed clay bowl, a sooty runny nostril blowing in and out, beady black and filmy. How much money has gone into this little eye, as more and more people were saying. It wheezed away, the tiny buzz buzz regularly spaced could be annoying. But no matter how expensive it was still under control, not like the abyss waiting for him outside the door. It held the family together. They had their own atmosphere here in the clouds of blue smoke, and this was home while the singsong houses were society to him.

She knew he would settle down to Dungmei. Smokers like to have everything close at hand. A cigarette tin lined with newspaper nestles beside the pillow to save the trouble of leaning over to use the spittoon. He did not even mind his wife's looks.

Dungmei had a permanent wave in the latest style called airplane head, with wings of tight curls set high on the sides of the head. Buxom in a red-trimmed gown of flowered silk she kotowed to him and went to kotow to his wife, being their joint property from now on. But it would be bad omen to kneel to someone in bed. Only corpses received obeisances lying down. The amahs stopped her.

'Just say it, it's the same.'

It was not, and gave her position another boost. Yindi had put her in the front room and gave her the best amah. She made her take charge of housekeeping and praised her to the skies. Yensheng's wife lying in the back room lacked everything. No doctors came any more. When her family in Wuweichow finally got word of it they asked a relative to call at the house and see their daughter. After the visit Yindi sat in her own doorway shouting for hours: 'Life is hard here, then don't marry into our house. More like an ancestor has come to stay! Want to go home, go and never come back again, thanks be to heaven and earth. I know Dungmei is the trouble, she's in the way. There're those that will straddle the latrine hole and not move their bowels, but won't let others get their turn. Endless fights for separate beds, so what's wrong with separate rooms? What did we want a daughter-in-law for, if not for carrying on the line, I'd like to ask our in-laws. They want to talk to us, good, we want to talk to the matchmaker too. Cheating with a photograph. Then palming a tubercular demon on us.'

She got into the habit of straddling a bench across the doorstep yelling in the direction of the sick room. Almost every day something touched it off. When Dungmei became pregnant she called out, 'If it's a boy she'll be set upright the minute the tubercular demon draws her last breath.' A concubine made a wife is 'set upright'.

The third child and second boy was born before the wife died. There was no more mention of setting anybody upright.

15

Sometimes she said to Yensheng, 'We get laughed at, as if we can't afford to get you another wife, or is it because my evil name is out and people won't give us their daughter?'

He said he didn't want one.

'He's had enough,' she explained to relatives. 'He's afraid of getting another one like that.'

As long as the position remained vacant she could always send for the matchmakers in case Dungmei got out of hand. She was big with child again, walking around with chest and stomach out, looking quite bold. She was no fool, she knew the more children the harder it would be for him to remarry. It put most people off to hear there was already 'somebody in the room', not to say a whole brood of heirs. The children were underfoot all the time but to move the lot of them downstairs would be letting Dungmei off too lightly, although there were times when she got on her nerves. There would be a word or a look as if between a married couple—not that Yensheng paid her much attention.

He didn't turn out badly. In fact he was smart enough in his quiet way on the few times they had to negotiate business to tide things over when money from the land was held up. She let him handle it, he could be trusted because he wanted to win her confidence. How long would he hold on to the things once out of her hands? She could only hope he would know better by then.

Her greatest satisfaction remained the relatives. Big Master had got into trouble a few years ago. The headlines had died down with still a paragraph in the

newspapers every now and then, the biggest embezzle-
ment case in the Nationalist régime. Relatives were hard
put to it to find anything to say. He only escaped jail by
going to hospital for his liver. A frame-up they said, by a
colleague who put the blame on him. She would call it
real retribution. So grasping at the division of property—
not so easy to do the same in the outside world. He was the
capable one, but he did not seem to know the old saying,
'Without connections at court don't be a mandarin.'

He kept appealing from his hospital sanctuary. The
trials were strung out for years passing from hand to hand
and all palms had to be greased. The costs came to a
fortune in debts. Ninth Old Master just made sympathetic
noises when Big Mistress went to kotow to him weeping
begging for help. After all he had brought it on himself.

He finally left hospital quietly, the case closed, part of
the missing funds paid. He died broke within the year.
Big Mistress packed up and moved to Peking where the
living was cheaper. They still had lots of relatives there
and everybody likes the Peking climate, dry and bracing.
The political climate was also more sympathetic, the north
had never quite belonged to the Nationalists.

'It's good up north,' Yindi said to her son. 'They say
the Japanese are all over the place now. If the Japanese
must come it couldn't be helped, it's another thing to
rush up to meet them.'

Quite a few families had moved away. The cost of
living was too high, especially the opium. It would be
embarrassing to keep moving to ever smaller places while
in the interior they could still live in style. Some even
moved to their land in the country and played squires,
knowing very well it was unsafe there.

'Their ancestors got them land and houses in Shanghai

and they have to go and live in bandit dens,' she said to Yensheng.

Signs of war with Japan frightened the new country squires into moving back again, paying exorbitant key money to rent a house. There was fighting in Shanghai too but it never got to the British or French settlements. She had to credit Third Master with more sense than these people, he hung on here for better or worse. Word came that one of his concubines had moved in with the other.

'They must really pinch and save now. Don't the two quarrel living together?'

'Leave it to Third Master, he's smart.'

'What does he live on nowadays?'

'His concubine has money.'

'And the other one? She supports her too?'

'Well, our Third Master is smart.'

'Not easy for him either, he's getting on now, and with a young master's temper like his.'

It was all speculation. Nobody had been to see him and his servants were not in touch with relatives' servants as they came from a different source, either recommended by his friends or brought over from the singsong house. With the growing blank over the years there was more respect for him. In their set there was an unspoken admiration for anybody able to fend for himself by fair means or foul without falling back on family or relatives.

'They say he never gets out of the house, not even downstairs.'

She remembered him saying, 'I seldom ever go out. Getting old, not welcome any more.' He had been barely forty then but without money was naturally not as popular as before. One thing about him, he was sensitive. Don't tell her he does not miss the fun and crowds because he is getting old, it's the only life he knows; or because he has company—two scoops of stale water out of the sea he loves. He just made himself as comfortable as he could in his hole and shut out prying eyes to have a clean quiet end, not unlike her there. She tried to give these people nothing more to talk about and seemed to hear an answering silence from him. Nobody knew what there had been between them and that grew with the years. She had a peculiar understanding for him like that between husband and wife, even when the wife knew nothing about her husband's business. It was a wonder that he was still himself after years of that wearing emptiness. She could stand it much better, being used to it, yet she sometimes did not act like herself. At least he had never tried to see her on the chance of some money. He knew it wouldn't be any use, he had said she was hard. He still remembered.

If there was some wishful thinking in her seeing him as being in the same boat, it so happened that more and more people were put into her position. When the Japanese finally took over the foreign settlements everybody who could afford it stayed home and 'doused their lights and nursed darkness' in the ancient tradition for evil times. Men did not go out to work, most jobs smacked of collaborating. So not just her relatives but all of the more scrupulous people had come to be like her, a widow who stayed home to keep watch over her chastity. Now she could pinch pennies legitimately as everybody was doing. She set Dungmei to work making briquettes, she made them rounder than the servants. She squatted in the backyard mixing it with mud, patting it into egg-shape with a spoon, her plaid cotton gown flung high behind above the ample bottom.

But she was not a good housekeeper. Yindi got so exasperated that she went down to the kitchen herself to show the cook how to save the rationed oil. Dip a writing brush in the bottle and draw a few strokes in the pan. Yensheng could not eat the vegetables fried like this, he had to have special dishes prepared for him upstairs. But she only saved where people could not see. The number of servants remained about the same, only the cook used to be a man, now they made do with a cook amah like most other families. At the Suns it was now Second Mistress Sun who 'went down to the stove' herself as if to the mines. They were a large family, always hard up and the old couple were still living. Dainty giggly little Second Mistress Sun whom she used to joke with would make her appearance towards the end of the dinner, slightly flushed but neat and hen-like, trying to be self-effacing, taking compliments with a murmured, 'Oh, were the shrimp balls all right?'

'Second Mistress Sun is so capable, she can cook a whole feast,' people marvelled behind her back, actually horrified. 'Just like in a restaurant, eggs scrambled as fine and even as fish scales, chopsticks cannot pick them up.'

In the occupied city each family had to contribute a man to stand guard in the neighbourhood. Those who had no manservants would hire a man by the hour. At the Suns it was Second Master Sun himself. Yensheng had happened to see him and described to her how Second Uncle Sun stood in front of the sentry box outside the alley, tall, thin and high-shouldered, chin up and half smiling cynically with his big tortoise shell glasses, a rope over one shoulder tied to the policeman's club slung low on his long gown.

They have too many mouths to feed, Yindi said, and we haven't got too many? Time was when they used to say her branch had so few people and even now hardly realized how much manpower she had. Her grandsons seldom appeared when there was company.

Nowadays when she was mentioned it was always, 'They still just have that Miss Dung?' smiling disgustedly with the face all screwed up. 'There's only her? Never remarried. How many children now?'

She was more criticized for not getting her son another wife than for maltreating her daughter-in-law which after all was the custom. But it was unheard of for a young widower to stay single for life.

She was angry when she heard of it. Trust these people always to have something to say. The year of the war in Shanghai her brother's family had been refugees from the Old City, so she had helped to resettle them in Hangchow where one of their sons had a job. With the shop gone she thought to give these people that much less to talk about. She knew their every inflection and flicker of expression, just let a few words reach her ears and she could see it all. That was her trouble, unable to pretend to be half blind and deaf like all the truly blessed old ladies. She admitted it herself.

Relatives who had moved away would ask grinning, when they came to town, 'Second Mistress is still like that? How is it we haven't heard about her all this time?'

'She's ill,' whispered almost defensively. 'She has gall-stones.' Her illness had given her new dignity, excusing her from all the gatherings that wouldn't have included her anyway.

'How are they doing now?'

'Oh, they're rich,' in a still lower whisper with a half-wink and nod.

'There's still just that Miss Dung? How many children now?'

There were so many, they all looked about the same

178

size, dark and squat with sturdy legs, in khaki shorts and canvas shoes. They went to an alley school near by. By the time it came to them everybody went to school. The family could only show their opinion of the system by choosing the nearest and cheapest. After they got home they chased each other downstairs from one room to another, but silently like a group of rats rolling heavily over the floor and back again. They had the run of the downstairs suites because their parents had moved downstairs. The dark rooms grown shabby and untidy had the air of a caretaker's apartment. The white sliding doors had yellowed unevenly like dental plates and had the same smell. It was dark enough to put the lights on in the afternoon but there was just the opium lamp on Yensheng's couch.

Dungmei pretended to straighten out the things on top of the bureau. She took a couple of steps forward seeing there was no one around and stood before his couch with a coltish awkwardness that sat oddly on her broad-beamed figure, the old sweater pulled awry at the back, stuck at the top of the bulge.

'No mention of coal money,' she blurted out petulantly in a low grunt without indicating upstairs with the least movement of the eyes or head which she held down stiffly.

Curled up on his side, hands tucked in his sleeves, looking coldly at the lamp, he made a small noise that meant he wanted no part of it. She turned to drive out the children rolling noisily into the room.

Yindi faced her own lamp upstairs. Because of illness she smoked in bed, not such an open place as the couch and less lonely with nobody lying opposite her. There was just the little slave girl sitting on the low stool in front of the bed cleaning the pipe bowl. There weren't slave girls any more, this one was just a child Old Cheng picked up, intended for her grandson when they grew up, which would be a saving. While waiting for some fellow countrymen to take her home she had permission to keep her here to help out. Little girls were often called Little Slave Girl in their part of the country, a convenient reminder to Dungmei. Yindi would sometimes purposely scold her a bit or give her a slap when Dungmei was around. Now that the singsong houses were enjoying a new boom, patronized by the hoarders, small businessmen that got rich quick, they had spoiled it for Yensheng. He had stopped going altogether, a good thing in itself, only he kept to his lairs downstairs more than ever. This Dungmei was too good a breeder. People laugh when it comes in litters like pigs. She was pennypinching only for the sake of the children's future. What was going to happen if this went on? Especially in times like these when money was not worth anything. A couple of years ago she used to give Yensheng thirty cents a day for pocket-money. Singsong houses used the credit system and settled three times a year. But he liked to take walks to get his own candies which most smokers seem to need, or to the street of antique stores to buy a little chipped bowl or an inscribed brick or half a seal-colouring box. There were trunkfuls of antiques at home that he had never even seen, but as long as it amused him . . . The thirty cents gradually rose to a dollar, two dollars. With the change of currency after the occupation it went steadily up to two hundred dollars, five hundred. This year nobody knew how much tips to leave at New Year visits. It had always been eight dollars from near relatives, ten at the most and two or four dollars from distant relatives. By rights everybody should have waited to see how much she gave so as not to top her, she was the oldest branch now that the eldest branch had moved away. She was angry and told them off through other relatives. Of the old ninth branch Ninth Old Master and his wife had both passed away and the son and daughter-in-law were younger than her. They were still the richest by far but as there had been talk that the son was not Ninth Old Master's, if he was not considered a real Yao then he did not count. That would leave just her branch, at least still keeping up appearances carrying on in the same house. Twenty years was as a day to them even if they flourished only in numbers. At least they wouldn't die out like the third branch. As for the eldest branch with their fanciful children, ruined as they were, the youngest daughter had to go and marry her teacher. Everything said about girls' schools would seem to be proved true. Big Mistress was unwilling but evidently unable to do anything about it. It must have been too late.

'Theirs is "teacher-pupil love",' people said smiling, using the new term. There were such cases. Nobody would say much about it. 'He first taught her in junior middle school,' they'd whisper, smiling sweetly, not quite looking each other in the face. So it had started when she was in her early teens.

'He resigned,' they said. There must have been a real scandal and this in the conservative north. 'Wu Hsichen has quite a temper,' they had learned after the marriage. He was always called by his full name like all peripheral relatives.

The second son now was married to a relative by family arrangement, only the young couple got on too well together. Second Young Mistress put her chin on his shoulder watching him play mahjong with his mother. Big Mistress couldn't get used to the sight, spoke to her about it and she got up and went to her own room crying, and straight away agitated for moving out to be on their own. Second Young Master was working as a government clerk in Peking. People just said, 'He found a small job,' and let it go at that.

Playing mahjong yet. All so normal.

'Big Mistress is pitiful now,' everybody said. She probably depended on what money her eldest sent her from Shanghai, the son that had been abroad. He had got on the good side of a vice-president of the new government bank, played the market with him and ran around with him and cabaret girls. It does pay to study abroad. His wife played mahjong with the wives of the puppet officials, as proud as could be. What would happen after Japan fell? It would not be long now, Germany was already defeated. She had to keep track of these things, anybody with land in the interior was affected by the wars. She pored over the old book of prophecy, *The Picture of Back Massagers*, little men sitting in a row massaging each other's back. Each had someone behind him doing what he did to the one before him. There were other drawings of the same childlike men in kimono jackets and trousers, one standing on the other's shoulders and in other mysterious poses, accompanied by cryptic verses. But the terror was confined to the pages of the thin little book. Whatever massacre or holocaust may come true, by the time it got to Shanghai the worst of it was rising prices. Didn't the fall of the Manchus count as a great calamity? And of course the coming of the Japanese. Once you have weathered through the Japanese, you need not be afraid no matter who comes. Shanghai is still Shanghai and it's not as if you poke your head out and show your face like Little Feng of the eldest branch. He thought he was clever to have got the benefits without taking a government post. Besides he probably thought he had nothing to lose after his father's scandal. His father's fling with the Nationalists was actually another asset with the régime here who particularly welcomed defectors from Chungking.

'So on the strength of his poor father and great grand-father he got to be Hsu Yuehting's hanger-on,' she had said to Yensheng.

'Little Feng is rich now,' people said smiling, using the same euphemism for official influence but their smiles were broader. Before, with all the changes of government since the republic it had still been one's own people, still polite to one another, it was never anything to get one's head chopped off for, not like now when you were called traitor. Really, compared to the pair of them in the eldest branch, father and son, Third Master didn't come off so badly. The only trouble with Third Master was he never looked ahead, not that she'd turn round and speak well of him now that he was dead. It had been a real shock, without hearing anything about him being ill. Only fifty-three—having got to this age herself she couldn't help feeling it counted as a short life. Of course he had ruined his health by being cooped up in the house all these years, never so much as stepping on the ground to get a breath of earth. And two concubines to keep him company and they weren't always pregnant either like this one of Yen-sheng's. Maybe it was just as well he died now while it could still be said that he'd had a good life, with two concubines to see him off at the end. In a few more years they would be old. There is hardly any point in growing old with two women. They were still staying together as his widows, presumably the one still supporting the other. She must say that was rare. He didn't end up so badly. If he had sunk too low she wouldn't have face either, after all with a woman——

Then she heard Old Mistress Sun had been to see his two concubines. The two lived in a tiny room between

183

floors in a little alley house, with no furniture other than
a bed.

'What is there to do all day long except to sit or lie
down?' they had said. 'We sit on the bed back to back.'

She was also aghast.

'How old are they?' she asked. 'One is younger than
the other, isn't she? Actually if anybody wants them why
not just go, although I shouldn't be saying this.'

Everybody was just as horrified to hear that Second
Master Liu and his brother-in-law had both got rid of their
thirty-year-old opium habit. It had just got too expensive
for them. There was always a moment of silence after the
news was whispered, smiling, embarrassed by such extremities. News came far in between but the days and months
were going so fast it seemed to her that endings caught
up with people quickly nowadays. Time was always on
her side. The worse the times the more it proved she was
right. It went faster and faster, stronger for being compressed, blowing by her ears with a roar. She could feel it
go, with a sudden chill running like a thread being pulled
down her back or sides, a little frightening but not a bad
feeling. Of course Third Master's death made her think
of herself and she was ill too but illness is just a thing
people have to carry around with them as they get on
in life.

She uncapped a stick of eucalyptus balm and rubbed it
on her temples enjoying the mint smell and the cold, that
felt like somebody else's thumbs pressed on her temples.
With the slight shift of position also came the odour of
old clothes and stale smoke and she nestled in deeper.
She picked up a pair of tweezers in the tray to pluck at
the lampwick and took the glass chimney off the pale
copper lamp base with cut-out patterns. The glass was hot,
somehow a pleasant surprise. Looking out from under the

184

bed curtains the room was larger and the ceiling higher than ever. The closed grey windows were a long way off. She wondered if it was already getting dark outside. The little slave girl was nodding—never had enough sleep day and night. She picked up the little lamp and brought the steady flame like a soy bean to the child's hand, all of a piece with the chubby wrist and the same width. The unexpectedly heavy parry as of a stumpy forefoot nearly knocked the lamp on the floor. It reminded her of the time she had burned a man's hand. Suddenly it all came back, the banging on the boarded shopfront, she standing right behind it, her heart pounding louder than that, the hot breath of the oil lamp in her face, her fringes coming down muffling the wet forehead and her young body picked out in the dark by the prickly beads of perspiration. Everything she drew comfort from was gone, had never happened. Nothing much had happened to her yet.

'Miss! Miss!'

Her name was being called. He was calling her outside the door.

Eileen Chang, 1966
Courtesy of Crown Publishing Company, Ltd., Taipei, Taiwan.